FIND
HIS
GRAVE

A totally gripping crime thriller full of twists

KATE WATTERSON

Detective Chris Bailey Series Book 4

Joffe Books, London
www.joffebooks.com

First published in Great Britain in 2023

Cover art by Nebojša Zorić

ISBN: 978-1-83526-037-1

PROLOGUE

The day I died, I saw it coming but was helpless to prevent it.

Dark night, close and warm, the insects humming their incessant tune, the very air sticking to my skin . . . I remember it well.

It had been building, a growing rift between two former friends, an unsaid argument, a situation neither one of us wanted to acknowledge.

A disagreement as old as time. Two men, one woman.

The irony of it was, I believe he understood my point of view, and I also understood his.

I swear I could smell it coming. Danger, fear, hate, envy, whatever you want to call it, the sum of the parts wasn't pretty. That emotion takes hold and digs in deep.

I saw the movement out of the corner of my eye, but by then it was too late. A figure loomed as I swung around, ready to defend myself, but not quite fast enough.

A night bird called in the distance, dissonant and melancholy. I remember the sound.

Disbelief swept over me as I saw the knife protruding from my chest.

I don't remember any pain, only a sense of disembodied realization of what had just happened, fatalistic knowledge that I had lost this battle and my enemy stood there, triumphant.

As I fell, I could hear him laughing.

That was the worst part of the whole experience.

CHAPTER ONE

Dreary day inside and out.

Gray skies outside just spitting rain, muggy and yet not all that warm. Detective Chris Bailey was tired of endless paperwork at this point, though it was done on the computer most of the time — no paper involved.

He had some down time in mind in the form of his cabin at the river, cold beer, and a couple of old John Wayne movies on DVD. Feet up on the old coffee table, his little dog for company — it sounded pretty nice. A ham sandwich for dinner was fine with him. He could manage that, or maybe grill a hamburger.

The phone on his desk rang. Most of the time people called his cell, so this meant department business. He picked up. "This is Bailey."

"What if I told you I know where his body is?"

Disembodied voice, no particular tone, no number provided. After a moment, Chris said evenly, "I believe I would ask you who we are talking about."

"I'll get back to you on that."

The caller hung up.

He just sat there, still holding the phone, feeling the anticipation of a relaxing few days evaporate.

What the hell was that about?

He got up and walked over to his partner's desk. Carter was like him, trying to wrap everything up before leaving for what should be an uneventful couple of days. They were always essentially on duty, but sometimes people behaved themselves, and they got a few days off. He sat down. "Do we have any pending missing person cases right now that involve a male?"

Carter was definitely a more seasoned detective, at least twenty years older. They'd formed a working relationship based more on a sense of trust, due to some interesting mutual experiences during a few tough cases, than a personal connection. In short, they had come to the conclusion that maybe listening to each other was a good idea, even if they didn't always agree.

"Why?" Carter pushed a key and closed his computer, his gaze sharply inquisitive.

"Strange phone call. I'm not quite sure what to make of it. All the person really said was they could tell me where 'his body', whoever that might be, was. It was odd too, as they phrased it in the form of a question. 'What if I told you I know where his body is?'"

Carter leaned back. "Okay, yeah, that's not the usual, I admit. We do get some pretty off-the-wall characters now and then, but usually Doreen handles them."

He was right. Doreen ran the sheriff's office, and she was frighteningly efficient. Chris thought about it. "This came right to my desk."

"So this person has your direct line."

"He knows me, or knows someone who does." There was no denying that. Not a random call. If they had just been calling the sheriff's office, they would have had to go through Doreen or the emergency response hotline.

If someone was already buried, it didn't sound like an emergency.

"Why do it?"

Carter raked his hand through his thinning hair. "There you go, asking the wrong question. 'Who' is the right way

3

to approach this, if you even want to approach it at all. We don't have a known victim."

Why was it Chris thought that a victim was out there? Grave deep.

* * *

The setting was interesting, anyway.

Whitney was interested in history, so the decrepit structure did intrigue her, but she really had no idea why she might be there. Abandoned southern mansion, old trees, the symbol of a decaying time, the roof speckled with lichen, the grounds overgrown but still a ghostly image of their former glory. This was Tennessee — not the Deep South, but at one time there were some substantial holdings here. There still were, actually, but this one had been forgotten a long time ago.

Why he had requested she meet him at this particular location, she wasn't sure, but Cal had been specific in his text. She hoped it wasn't because he was thinking of buying this property. The cost of demolishing the house alone would be prohibitive, but maybe he had an investor. Her brother was progressive when it came to business. Construction was his specialty and he was good at it.

Except, when he pulled up the rutted driveway, he got out of his expensive SUV and looked around. "What do you think?"

They were brother and sister, but though there was a familial resemblance in the unusual color of their eyes, no one would ever guess it. He was a good foot taller and his hair was curly, not irritatingly straight like hers, and his affable smile usually drew attention, where she tended to be far more reserved.

She said succinctly, "If someone wanted to film a horror movie, this would be a great location."

He was unfazed. "Or, if someone wanted to make it into a very nice and fairly pricey hotel, set in a scenic part of Tennessee, it might be perfect, right?"

So that was it? Interesting idea.

"If you had a billion dollars. That driveway alone would give anyone pause." Why had she known that was what he had in mind? "What prompted this? I didn't even see a realty sign."

"It is on the historical register. I might need your help. You're an architect."

That was true enough. She did have a master's degree in architecture, but she didn't work on restoring old buildings. "I have no experience in what you want. The firm I work for mostly does newbuilds."

He put his hands in his pockets and looked thoughtful, staring at the building. "Look, you have connections. I have someone who really agrees with me this might be a lucrative idea. This place went up for sale for a song and you didn't see a sign because according to the realtor, someone stole it quite some time ago. I only stumbled across the listing by accident because I was looking for land and saw the acreage, which was how they were marketing it. We'd be paying for the location, that's it most of all, but the house has character. It just needs to be expanded, and yet adhere to the time period when it was built."

Well, that sounded about right, because as far as she could see, the house was falling down. "So, no restoration?"

"We will use what we can, of course, but need plans to rebuild a lot of it. I think we'd like it to resemble the original structure enough to keep the historical designation."

That she could do. Whitney was starting to see the vision. "Okay, I can probably help with that."

"I figured you could."

"The historical society might have photographs at least, or even the original drawings."

"They do; we've checked. And when we hire a licensed architect, they will gladly loan them out to that person."

She raised a brow, assessing the size of the house and the somewhat daunting scope of the project. Yet here she was on this muggy day, standing in what barely passed for a drive-way, it was so rutted and in disrepair. "I'm 'that person'?"

"How it will work is, we handle the money and the construction process; you handle the design, inside and out, and the historical part of it."

She got it. It was not an original idea, but it was the kind of concept that had worked out for other people with a vision, along with the money and savvy to do it. Which was exactly Cal's area of expertise, since he had a degree in construction management.

"The landscaping? I would have no idea."

"We'll hire a company for that. An arborist first, and then the muscle to get it done, but the house is the main concern. Are you in?"

It was intriguing, and of course she loved her brother, but she wasn't positive she had the time. "Are you hiring me or the firm?"

"If I have to go through the firm, I will, on the proviso you handle it. I know I can work with you."

"Who else are you working with on the project?" A logical question she'd ask anyone.

Cal furrowed his brow. "Ross. He's pretty well known for being a canny business guy, and we graduated together after being roommates in college. He's intelligent and I trust his judgment, not to mention he's gathering investors. He's way better at that than I am. I can manage the project, and he'll come up with the money. When he heard you were licensed as an architect, he signed on."

"You told him I'd do it and asked me after the fact." A statement, not a question.

"Pretty much." Her brother looked unrepentant, even amused.

"Why am I assuming now you've already bought it?"

"Well, we've literally known each other all our lives." He took the keys out of his pocket and held them up. "Honestly, this is a great investment."

It probably was. No illusions there. Her brother had a keen eye for unique opportunities. Even as a child, his business acumen was evident. Their parents had laughed about it, and yet steered him in that direction after he organized a neighborhood lawn-mowing enterprise that did quite well, considering he was all of ten years old at the time.

She did not have — or understand — that skill set. But she could look at a building or a piece of land and picture the possibilities in a different way.

"Well," she said, "let's go inside and check it out."

The front porch was so unstable and unsafe she was afraid to walk across it, but careful attention meant neither of them went through any rotting boards. The first thing she noted was the graceful beauty, antebellum style, of the formal front entrance . . .

And then the blood.

Cal didn't need his keys; the front door was ajar, a glossy trail of scarlet droplets gleaming in the fading afternoon light.

Whitney stopped cold, glancing over at her brother and registering the same consternation in his expression. He muttered, "What the hell? Stay here."

She caught his arm. "Don't go in there."

"I believe we just established this is my house." He pulled free and used his foot to shove open the door. "Let me see what's going on. For all we know, a coyote killed a rabbit and carried it in here for his evening snack."

That might fly, she thought, but no predator besides a human being would be able to unlock and open a door.

Stale air, dust, and silence.

Of course, she followed him in. Like she'd let her brother walk into whatever might have happened in his deserted purchase alone.

Some of the furnishings were still there, like dusty symbols of faded generations long gone: a built-in china cabinet with broken glass in one corner near a massive fireplace, two dusty ornate chairs in a corner, a grandfather clock without hands . . .

And a large pool of congealed blood.

"That would have to be a very big rabbit." She said it not to be sarcastic, but because she was uneasy. There had to be an explanation, but she wasn't positive she wanted to know what it was.

Cal stared at the floor. "Yeah. Why is it I'm doubting that's the explanation after all? Rabbits don't have hands."

It was true, she saw, with a chill that rippled through her entire body. There was a very clear bloody imprint of a human hand on the scratched hardwood floor.

CHAPTER TWO

As I look back on the events that escalated from unfortunate to cata-strophic, there is clarity of vision in my role in the entire drama.

Arrogance is not a useful character flaw, but I had it in full measure. I won't say it was the death of me, but it certainly played a vital part.

Let's say I refused to acknowledge my weakness and my enemy took great joy in my blindness.

She wasn't without guilt, either. This was not one-sided. He bore some of the responsibility for what happened, but not all of it.

* * *

There was no doubt he wanted it all: the success and the money were nice, but mostly Ross Waylan wanted the girl.

Age-old problem.

A part of him wished he'd never seen her, when he was about twenty, for the first time. What an interesting dilemma for a man who considered himself reasonably sophisticated. He and Cal had become friends already, but meeting his sister had been a memorable event. She was reserved, poised and memorably lovely — that was the poetic term he would use — and it was possible he'd been struck by the proverbial arrow.

He sat at his desk and thought about it. There were some things that came with a price he wasn't sure wasn't too high. For one, a business relationship was involved, and that was usually a damn bad idea. He had his faults, but he liked to think that poor judgment wasn't one of them.

So when the phone rang, he wasn't sure if he wanted to hear if Whitney Nolte accepted the job or not. If it was a yes, they'd be working together. A true ironic conflict of interest.

It turned out that the call had nothing to do with that.

"Ross, we have a very odd problem. You know, the kind you never see coming down the pike."

No greeting, no other particular courtesy, but in Cal Nolte's defense, they knew each other well. "What odd problem?"

"I think I need to call the police, but I'm not sure. Isn't your cousin a cop?"

That was not how he ever wanted to start a conversation. "Yes . . . what's going on?"

There was a hesitation, and then Cal said simply, "I went to show Whitney the house, and there's blood on the floor. I looked through the place and that's it. No evidence I can see of an actual crime, just a pool of blood. I mean, I feel I should call law enforcement, but to report what? That lock on the front door could be original. I could probably open it with a toothpick, and being a burglar is hardly in my skill set."

He thought about it. "I can see why emergency services aren't necessary, but that's weird, man, I admit. What the heck? Someone break in and decide to sacrifice a chicken or something?"

Nolte said dryly, "Nary a feather. I went for a coyote–rabbit encounter, but Whitney pointed out it'd have to be quite a big rabbit. It's a substantial amount of blood, and there's a handprint that has to be human."

That changed the game in an ominous way.

Not to mention, they didn't need to try to launch a project like turning a house into a hotel if something gruesome had happened there.

"I'll call Jamie right now and get his advice on how to handle it."

His cousin was off duty but answered his cell. He listened, and then his first comment wasn't encouraging. "Given the location, the county boys need to handle this. Just call the sheriff's office. You'll get Doreen, and she will know who should come take a look, where they are, and how soon they can get there. Tell Nolte not to touch anything."

"He's far too smart for that. Okay, thanks."

He called, got the said Doreen, who handled it so efficiently he felt like he was fifteen, instead of a grown man with a desk and a real occupation. Then he decided maybe he should go look for himself.

Or was it possible he wanted just to see Whitney?

He was worried that conflicted feelings might be involved and his motivation was not altruistic. He called Cal back, told him he was on his way and law enforcement was aware of the issue, then shut down his computer and headed to his car.

He was going to have to deal with it. It was fine to have an interest and not so much to have obsession. He did have a tendency to focus too much, but so far it had never extended to the opposite sex. He'd mostly had casual and uncomplicated relationships that were severed the minute he started to sense too much involvement. He liked attractive women, and it seemed they liked him back, but "sexual" was fairly close to his limit. His sister had pointed out more than once it was possible he had commitment issues.

So dial it back.

Could he?

He wasn't sure.

Part of his problem was this: did Whitney realize he was interested in the first place? If not, that could be his fault, because while he got his points across well in the business world, he wasn't sure he was good at interpersonal communication.

* * *

The old mansion wasn't that far from town, which made it ideal for a hotel, private grounds but with dining and shops close by. With the slanting shadows and winding roads, it still took him almost a half an hour to get there. He winced as his sports car bumped up the uneven drive.

He parked next to Cal's vehicle, got out, eyed the sagging porch, and wondered not for the first time if he'd survive the trek across it. But the contractor was supposed to start the minute the permits were cleared, so replacing that hazard was first on the agenda.

So he braved the rickety boards and didn't crash through and break a leg. He saw the blood spatter before he gained the door.

It did not get better.

The gory mess in the formal foyer did not speak of a happy event. "Jesus," he muttered.

Cal stood well away from the evidence. So did Whitney, ethereally enchanting in the dim light, wearing a skirt and a silk blouse, her pale hair loose around her shoulders.

He really wanted to run his fingers through that silky hair, but not while staring at a congealing puddle of blood.

"I do see why this might catch your attention." Ross skirted it very carefully. "Don't worry, Doreen said someone would be here soon."

"Doreen?" Cal said.

"My new friend at the sheriff's office . . . I don't know her last name. You looked everywhere? This is a big house, which is why it will make a successful hotel."

"Not the basement. I don't think anyone without bloodhounds could find someone down there. There are no lights."

Whitney murmured, "Maybe we need some silver bullets."

"Aren't those for werewolves?"

Whitney gave him a tremulous smile. "If this project involves a decaying house with bloody floors, werewolves seem a distinct possibility."

He looked at her, trying to not betray that what he was really doing was admiring the delicate shape of her arched brows, her straight nose, and the soft curve of her lips. It was out of character for him to be so thrown by a woman that he lost his train of thought. He consciously brought himself back into the moment. "Does that mean you've agreed to take on the job?"

* * *

The situation was far from comical, but she had an urge to stifle an incredulous laugh.

Seriously? Had Ross Waylan just asked her that question?

Dark hair, dark eyes, a lean build and a confident air — he was intense and sharply intelligent, if Whitney had to define him. Strikingly attractive, with a very rare flashing smile, but he was a man who had a purpose for everything he did, and she was never quite sure how to take him. He and Cal were close friends, so she'd known him for a while, but there was the problem that she wasn't sure she knew him at all.

Very clear guidelines would have to be laid down if she chose to do this, because she had a feeling his keen eye would be on everything.

"I think I see your and Cal's vision, but the more immediate problem needs to be addressed first, and I think they just arrived."

It was true: there was the sound of a car door slamming. Cal said, "Let's hope no one weighs three hundred pounds or anything, or the porch will give."

Not the case. The man who gingerly pushed open the door that had been left ajar was tall but young and nicely built, and he looked nothing like a police officer except he had a badge pinned to his casual shirt, and a holstered gun. "I'm Detective Bailey. Doreen told me about your call. I see why you contacted us. This is interesting, for sure."

She had to agree. Walking into a deserted house and finding a fairly large pool of blood was probably of interest to a detective.

Cal introduced himself, and so did Ross, but she simply stood back from the interaction. It wasn't a desire to just let the men handle it, but more a feeling she was, so far, a mere onlooker.

The truth was, she might just turn down the job.

There was this glimmer of interest in Ross Waylan that alarmed her. She would swear he wasn't her type, and would also swear she wasn't his, either. The idea of working with him raised all kinds of the wrong flags, not because she wasn't one hundred per cent sure it would be lucrative, but it might be dangerous.

On a personal level, anyway.

"I'm going to look around," Bailey said. "Is the electricity off?"

Ross nodded. "The service needs to be brought up to code. This place is probably going down to the studs as we rebuild. This is a beautiful old house, but the keyword there is 'old'. It was built before the Civil War, and any and all improvements were piecemealed in by different generations of owners."

Whitney didn't disagree with him there. Good bones, but not necessarily salvageable. However, she could see the appeal. It could be perfect for a small, chic, and exclusive hotel in a beautiful place, a pool and spa of course, an outside dining area — plenty of space for that.

Maybe she wouldn't turn it down.

"I looked around when it was still light out and didn't see anything." Cal shook his head. "I looked in every room, but the flashlight on my phone isn't good enough for the basement."

"I'm not a forensic tech, but it seems to me whatever happened occurred right here, then the victim was carried out; that's why there's blood on the porch. That handprint is pretty disturbing."

She agreed entirely. The sight of it certainly had not improved her evening.

"Who else has access to this property?" The detective had his phone out and was texting someone, but still asking questions.

"Legal access? No one. But as long as it sat empty, I wouldn't be surprised if there were trespassers." Ross looked about as unhappy as her brother. He was still in his shirt and tie from work, but then again, she was also overdressed for an abandoned old house where something suspicious had happened. It was like she'd stepped into a melodramatic period play.

All they needed was a good thunderstorm to up the eerie ambiance, but it was a clear night, though it was getting dark in the unlit house.

"Well, me either." Detective Bailey was evidently a straightforward man. "Empty house, a place to sleep . . . there are some people around these parts who have either fallen on hard times or choose to ignore the laws of the state of Tennessee. I think, given the situation, maybe more officers should take a look. Sheriff Lawrence agrees."

There was more to this than Whitney had at first realized. She wouldn't say Bailey was expressive, but his face told her there was something about this place he wasn't saying.

"Has there been trouble here before?" It was the first she'd spoken since he arrived. She wasn't positive she wanted the direct attention, but she asked anyway.

He had striking blue eyes and a very direct focus. "I haven't had to pay a visit to this location before, but that isn't to say there haven't been previous calls."

In other words, a deputy, not a detective, would usually answer a vague call about some blood on the floor of a deserted house. Yet, instead, he'd taken an interest in it.

She had to wonder why.

And he'd called the sheriff to ask for more investigators?

This was not turning out to be the evening she expected.

Ross asked, "Would you prefer us to just get out of your way? Whitney is only here because she's our architect. And the two of us, other than previously walking through the house and reading the inspection report, we don't know much more than you do, if anything."

The reply was interesting. "I would like to know how to get in touch with all three of you, if you don't mind."

Ross handed over a business card. "Don't bother to lock up. Apparently anyone can get in, and there's nothing to steal so just shut the door when you leave, and maybe you can let us know what happened?"

"Oh, we'll be in touch. The police do things like that." Detective Bailey wore a cynical smile. "Feel free to go. This might or might not be a crime scene, but we will process it that way. So unless you have more to tell me, you'd just be standing around."

They walked out to their cars, carefully navigating the porch and crumbling steps. A night bird called from some- where, distantly.

"I'm going to go home and drink a very tall beer." Cal meant it; she could tell. He looked at her. "I'm sorry this evening was a waste of your time, but think about this pro- ject, please, and hand us some ideas."

"I will," she promised.

"Good. Right now I'm getting the hell out of Dodge before more vehicles pull up. The driveway is too narrow for squeezing around cars."

Ross walked with her the few feet to her car and politely opened her door. "Have dinner with me?" He immedi- ately shook his head. "That wasn't exactly smooth. Let me rephrase. If you don't already have other plans, I'd like to take you out to dinner."

CHAPTER THREE

I think childhood was a blurred image of what I expected it to be. I thought of riding ponies and swimming holes, but it ended up like living in an armed camp. Hate is a powerful motivation; one must manage it carefully.

Desire became a complication that blurred the edges.

At least mine did.

I started something I was never meant to finish.

* * *

Why it never got easier was a mystery to him, but in general women were hard to understand, so asking someone out on a date was like strapping on some skates and taking a spin on thin ice.

Whitney didn't look all that surprised, which meant Ross's interest had been noticed. The real question was if it was returned. After a moment, she did ask, "Business or personal?"

"No mention of old houses with bloody floors, if that's your preference. You have my word."

He found the soft curve of her lips promising. "That sounds good to me."

"We'll be overdressed, but like Cal, I could use a cold beer. There's a place close to here that's small, but pretty down-home Tennessee. I'm even going to toss out the word 'quaint'."

"I actually have no objection to 'quaint', so fine with me."

Which meant, I have no objection to some time with you.

"Then follow me?"

"Let's go." She lowered herself into her car. "I'm with Cal: that driveway is barely passable."

He got in his car and drove — carefully — down the long twisty lane and headed toward the Tanglewood Tavern. It did a prosperous business, which was encouraging for the hotel. But he'd promised no business talk, and he planned to stand by it.

If ever there was a chance to catch her interest, maybe this was it. To sit down, share a drink, and firmly not talk business.

Or about this interesting situation.

The small parking lot was near full, but they each managed to find a spot, and there was a stroke of luck that he appreciated, considering his afternoon, in the form of an empty corner table. There were some appreciative male stares when Whitney walked through the crowded room.

His was one of them.

Frankly, he was the envy of every man in the room as he followed her to the table, pulled out a chair to seat her, and took an opposite seat. A harried waitress came by and Whitney ordered a glass of Chardonnay while he asked for a dark beer. This evening called for something stouter than a light lager.

"So how is the world of architecture?"

"Rather busy."

"Too busy?"

She gave him an amused look. "How did I know this would involve business?"

"Not at all," he contradicted smoothly. "That was personal."

He won that round. She looked chagrined. "Oh." After a moment, she said, "Point taken. Assume nothing?"

"I'm not just business."

"Says the only man in a tie and tailored slacks in a joint like this." Her expression reflected amusement.

"Joint?"

"I speak the vernacular."

"You're from around here, then?"

"So are you."

At least the banter was lighthearted, compared to the reality of what they'd just seen, and the realization that this business venture they were going to embark on might be a crime scene. Their drinks arrived, and the waitress departed with a promise to be back soon.

Whitney looked reflective as she picked up her wineglass and took a sip. "What do you think happened?"

It was a legitimate question. He also took a drink and pondered it. "Secluded location and an empty house . . . who knows? Cal is right. You could probably push that door open using just your hand."

"I guess I'm wondering why anyone would go there at all."

He'd been wondering that, too. Ross said slowly, "Now that I'm sitting here and thinking about it, when Cal and I looked at the place, I noticed a few things that made me wonder if someone might be living there, or maybe I should say camping out there."

"Like what?" Whitney looked interested, her glass suspended in her slender fingers.

She had amazing eyes, not quite blue and not quite green either. Aquamarine might be accurate.

"Some cans of food in one of the kitchen cupboards with no dust on them." He cast back, thinking it over. "I also noticed it seemed like one of the bedrooms upstairs looked like maybe it was being used. The floor had scuff marks, there were tumbled blankets and the window was open about halfway. Keep in mind, I wasn't paying a lot of attention, because I didn't know when the owners left. I was checking out the potential of the property more than anything. Plus, that was a while ago."

"That's interesting. I think maybe the detective might want that information."

He said wryly, "I would have told him, if I'd remembered it before now. I think the whole bloody handprint thing threw me off. The stuff I saw on the walk-through, I didn't realize the significance until now."

"Would the former owners know?"

The answer to that was easy enough. "I doubt it. Cal and I bought it from the bank. My understanding is a young couple bought it from the estate when the last close family member died, but before they could fix it up, they went their separate ways. Neither one could take on the mortgage on their own, so they threw up their hands and walked away. Three years on the market. That's why the bank sold it to us so under value, and why we had such a fast closing. We made a low offer, and they didn't even counter."

Maybe that would reassure her the scope of the project was doable. He knew they were a little young to embark on something as ambitious as this, but if she'd agree on a percentage basis to do the design, it would be good for the potential success of the project. He had an elite business degree, Cal had the expertise in construction management, and she was an architect that could design the dream.

Investors seemed to like the idea.

He did, too.

There was no doubt in his mind that they could pull it off. Hopefully Whitney agreed.

She said, "So you're convinced this will work."

"Yes, if we do it right."

The waitress came back then to take their order, stopping the conversation momentarily. Shrimp for her, a steak for him. After, he wondered if he should pursue the subject, but then, he had promised to not talk business.

So he chose to go back to personal. "So what happened to Darren, or was it Daryl? I think I only met him once."

She gave a slight grimace. "I don't know. Not to sound too unfeeling about it, but we were just casually dating anyway. The underlying problem might have been mine, but I found him boring. Good-looking guy, but it pretty much stopped there. Maybe other women find him fascinating, but I didn't. There was a hint of sexism there, too, in that he told me more than once it was odd for a woman to want to become an architect."

He laughed. "I think history will show that men have forever been afraid women might just be every bit as smart as they are, or maybe more so, and therefore support the idea that certain occupations should be kept in separate male/female categories."

Her brows lifted. "And you?"

"Trust me, if I was in a burning building and a female firefighter arrived, I would fling myself into her waiting arms."

It was her turn to laugh. "I'm sure you would."

"Damn straight." He grinned.

* * *

Why was it she wasn't positive this dinner was a good idea, but Whitney was glad she'd agreed.

If — *if* — they were going to work together, an attraction factor could be a problem.

After leaving what possibly could be the scene of some sort of dramatic event she didn't even want to imagine, she preferred to worry about something else. A complicated business decision seemed a good choice.

"Can you tell me what you have in mind?" She took a sip from her glass, gazing at him inquiringly.

He looked amused. "Okay, you're definitely going to have to clarify that question for me. I can come up with quite a few different answers, depending on the actual topic."

He tended to disconcert her, and she wasn't usually that way around men.

So she regrouped. "I meant, can you tell me about the plans for the house?"

"Oh, I see. Disappointed, but willing to cooperate. You're the professional, so tell me what you want to know."

That she could handle much better than how the lighting accented his cheekbones and dark hair and charismatic smile. "How many rooms, what size . . . I assume all that needs to be altered, since each room needs its own bathroom. And, do you want a pool out back, or an onsite restaurant? Plenty of details to be addressed."

"I can send you the plans I proposed to the investors. Until Cal talked to you, I wasn't sure if you'd be on board or not. He was, but I wasn't."

That meant he was perceptive. She wasn't sure her brother was right, either. "I'm fairly new to my firm, so my time is limited for an outside project like this."

"But you are thinking about it."

"I am, but I need to know the scope."

"Well, there must be a third floor, for one. It's a big house, but to become a small hotel, we'll need more rooms. Yes to the restaurant, of course, and a pavilion area for weddings or receptions. I'll hire someone for the pool design, because I wouldn't expect that from you. The marketing plan is in place. All we need is you."

It was easy to see why people might invest at his suggestion; he was succinct and confident. "I've never done anything like this on my own before," she pointed out.

"Life is full of those moments. Like taking the training wheels off your bike."

"Ross," she said wryly, "you just sounded like my father."

"Oh hell," he muttered, rubbing his jaw. "Worse than that, I think I just sounded like *my* father. You get the point, though. I haven't ever started a business venture like this one before, either. Nor has Cal."

"The three of us careening down the hill on two wobbly wheels? Does that sum it up?"

"Pretty much, except I think we all worked rather hard on gaining the skills to maneuver the bumps along the way and keep our balance."

"I think we're getting a little poetic, considering country music is playing in the background."

"Oh come on, this is Tennessee, darlin'. Of course there is."

His exaggerated drawl was effective and humorous; that side of him didn't surface often enough, in her opinion.

"I'm aware of where we are, and that it is a beautiful area, and I agree your idea just might fly."

"So you're in, bloodstained floors and all?"

"I thought you promised no bloodstained floor comments."

"Unless you wanted to talk about it."

He had a point. "Let's just hope you didn't buy a haunted house and the walls didn't just start to bleed."

"That might make me rethink this whole thing, but I'm going to assume that's not the case. I'm a bit skeptical of the whole paranormal angle. People are a lot more dangerous than ghosts."

There was no doubt she agreed. "That's probably the ugly truth."

From the jukebox, Patsy Cline declared she was crazy, and Whitney had to wonder if she was, too. "I'll draw up plans if you give me a solid idea of what you want."

"No problem." He lifted a brow. "That sounds like a deal?"

"I'll give it my best."

"I know that. It's why I want you."

Maybe it was her imagination, but she thought there was a double meaning in that statement and gave him a guarded look of inquiry.

In return, he added unrepentantly, "You are very qualified."

This was why she never knew how to take him. "Because I have a master's degree in architecture and I'm licensed?"

"That too."

His smile could be engaging when he chose to use it. Maybe it was just as well he didn't very often.

She set down her wineglass. "You are so hard to read sometimes."

"Let me be clear, then. I think you are both bright and beautiful." His gaze was intent.

Their salads arrived in time to cut off any reply she might make.

He was rather beautiful as well, in a purely masculine way with his clean-cut features and wavy dark hair, but she doubted he'd appreciate the compliment if phrased that way.

Sex with him would probably be an intense experience. That it even crossed her mind was both interesting and unsettling.

Even worse was that she was fairly sure he knew he had that effect on her.

It was difficult to be at a disadvantage. There was a definite difference in their scope of experience; that she knew already. He was only a few years older — he and Cal had met through their fraternity in college — but just from the handful interactions they'd had she knew he was somewhat of a player, and it was not her game.

The food was impressively good, which made an argument for the success of the enterprise, and when he told her the owner of the restaurant was investing in the hotel and enthusiastic about the idea, it didn't surprise her.

"His daughter is going to culinary school," Ross told her, a faint expression of satisfaction on his face when she praised their meal. "First of all, if she is half as good at this as Jon is, we will have a chef. And second, what better advertising for the hotel itself than this place?"

"You think of everything, don't you?"

"'Everything' is a bit too generous." He took a sip of beer. "But I think about a lot of things, and one of those things is you."

CHAPTER FOUR

It all started years ago. It was a small disagreement that grew like a weed in a stagnant pond; the muddy water made the actual cause difficult to remember.

A decaying friendship made for a very unhealthy competition.

It was even difficult to determine, when I thought about it, who was right and who was wrong, but it was the abhorrent behavior of my adversary that made me despise him so much.

Perhaps he would say the same of me.

Between the two of us was born a small but intensely violent personal war.

* * *

Sheriff Lawrence was a no-nonsense man. Pragmatic and blunt, he didn't spend a lot of time skirting around a topic. "So, what you're telling me is you have a possible crime scene, but no crime."

Since that did sum it up, all Chris could do was lift his shoulders in a shrug. "Yeah. I fully feel it is a crime scene, but no, I don't have a body. Yet someone offered me one."

Carter helped him out. "That phone call had some purpose."

"This is a new one on me. Is this like Jack the Ripper sending notes in the old days? 'By the way, I've killed someone, let's see if you can catch me'?"

They were in Lawrence's office, which always smelled like bitterly strong coffee and a hint of whiskey. The man did work long hours.

Chris shifted in his chair, restless and disturbed. "I'm pretty sure I don't like this game. Whoever called said he'd be in touch."

"No report of anyone recently gone missing?"

"None."

"Deserted house and a possible murder . . . drug deal gone wrong, maybe." Lawrence sounded resigned. "Those people do not play nice. It would be a convenient place for them to make a deal."

The only problem with that theory — to Chris anyway — was they usually did not call a detective with the sheriff's office to announce their crime. So something was really off. "I don't think so. He sounded . . . polished."

"Son, define that for me." Lawrence looked like he always did, skeptical.

"Well-educated."

"No hillbilly drawl, is what you're saying."

He thought back. "It wasn't a long conversation, but I'd more say he had a soft Southern accent. Generally, you're correct — not a usual roughneck."

The sheriff folded his hands and put his elbows on his desk. "Well, I'm just going to let you two keep me posted on this situation, because without a real crime to investigate, you have other things to do. But I agree we can't ignore it either."

They walked back to their desks. Carter said, "I'll admit I'm not sure we can do anything until your good friend calls you back as promised, if — and we have to say *if* — that call is connected to the blood in the empty house."

"I certainly think the timing would be interesting if it wasn't."

Chris settled back at his desk, sat down, and spotted the note by his computer.

What the hell?

Doreen's handwriting. *Someone left a message: "Not six feet deep"*.

He got up and walked over to the front desk. The office manager glanced up and gave her usual greeting. "What, sweetheart?"

Today she wore a new shade of lipstick. He actually noticed it. "Can I get some background to this message?"

"Like what? I wrote it down verbatim. Four words, that was it."

He was impressed she knew *verbatim*. "A person just called and you knew it was for me . . . how?"

"No, he asked for you when I answered your phone, and I explained you were in a meeting. He asked me to tell you that."

She'd been doing this a lot longer than him. He leaned against her desk. "Did he happen to leave a number?"

"Nope, but I have it."

Of course she did. Doreen was a wizard in magenta lipstick. She expounded, "Even when it says 'name unknown' I always write the number down. It doesn't mean it is traceable, but you can call it. Can I say that is one creepy message?"

"This particular individual seems good at that. Slow calm voice?"

"That describes it."

"Thanks, Doreen."

Her phone rang then, so he walked away, perturbed and unfortunately not sure what exactly to do next. Someone could just be getting off on making cryptic phone calls, but still . . . the timing.

However, it was impossible to look into it without some evidence. Yes, they'd collected a blood sample to see if they could get DNA, but even if they did, it took time, and the chances of it matching known DNA were like throwing darts at a blank wall.

So it seemed all he could do was wait and see what happened next.

He did drop off the note at Carter's desk. "As promised, he touched base."

After a swift read, his partner looked up. "What does this mean?"

"Carter, how the hell would I know? What I'm trying to decipher — and yes, I used that word — is why he'd want to draw attention to himself."

"You know I don't try to understand why, I just try to arrest who." Carter shook his head. "Ask your psychologist girlfriend about the motivation aspect, not me."

He had a point, and a lot more experience, though Chris had a decade in law enforcement under his belt now. "Anna is pretty insightful."

"She's pretty, all right."

Chris was always startled when Carter made any remark even remotely personal. He was a serious man who also took his job seriously. "I agree."

"So are you going to ask her?"

"I'll see what she thinks. Good suggestion."

"No. To marry you."

Where the hell did that come from?

It took him a moment, but the light dawned. "Is there some sort of office pool on that? You people need to get a life."

Carter simply leaned back in his chair, completely unrepentant. "Doreen started it."

It was Chris's turn to shake his head. "No insider information is available. I'm going back to my desk. Just thought I'd let you know there was another call."

"I'm just glad he's fixated on you and not me."

"Just my luck." He went back and sat down, pondering that message. *Not six feet deep.* Did that imply a shallow grave? As per his usual habit, he wrote it down. The process seemed to work for him. He made notes for each case and could refer back and adjust his thinking as he gained more information.

In this case, he had almost none.

Blood. A grave. And apparently, it wasn't six feet deep.

He called Anna. "I think I need therapy and Chinese food."

She didn't miss a beat. "I'm sure both of those things are true, but if this is a dinner invitation, you might want to reconsider your suave approach."

"Okay, let me put it another way, I'll pick up dinner and you can listen to me talk out loud and give me feedback. Better?"

"Marginally, but yes."

"My place or yours?"

"Yours is fine. I'm buried in work. Seven?"

"Sounds good."

* * *

Anna Hernandez pulled up to the house late, but if there was one thing she knew about her eclectic love affair, it was that Chris would not really notice, nor would he care if the food was a little cold because she was late.

They were a lot alike, which was a mixed bag in a relationship. Both of them were absorbed in demanding jobs, and therefore inclined to understand that in other people. On the flip side, intimacy for them was more about sharing a bed than sharing their lives.

However, it was nice to have an attractive man to have dinner and great sex with fairly often, so she was reasonably happy with the relationship as it stood.

And his cute little dog was a bonus. He called her Moppet, and she had long hair and questionable lineage, but she was sweet and always greeted Anna's arrival with enthusiasm, leaping up and down.

Chris was frowning at his computer when she walked through the door, but he did get politely to his feet, took the bottle of wine from her hands, and gave her a very nice kiss.

That was an improvement to her otherwise not-so-great day.

He felt solid and secure, and she actually needed that from time to time, so she lingered for a moment against him.

He felt it. "You okay?"

"I am now."

"Tough day, huh?"

"Very."

She'd had to remove five children from an abusive home. It was absolutely necessary; the wife was terrified to leave but also terrified to have them there, so she'd reported it. No clear-thinking human being with an ounce of compassion would have ever left the children in that situation, but Anna hated taking those kids from their mother. She was not the problem.

"I need you to talk to the sheriff about a certain man. Can you do that?"

Chris stared at her. "Well, of course. What's he done?"

"She won't press charges, so I had to recommend taking her children away."

"You're sure she won't press?"

"One hundred per cent."

"Okay. Can we charge him on anything else? What does she know?"

"Good question. I don't think she'd tell me."

"Because he'd retaliate? I think I can have a conversation with him to prevent that. Let me talk to her, and maybe she can get her children back. I can take Carter with me. He's really not about violence against women. I'm not either, of course, but with him it seems personal. I'm not sure what happened to make him that way."

She looked at him curiously. "He doesn't want to talk about it?"

"Anna, I haven't asked."

"A woman would just ask."

"In case you haven't noticed, I'm not a woman."

"I have noticed." She touched his face.

"Good. I made an impression."

"Yes, you have."

Nice second kiss.

He gestured at the kitchen. "I did my usual elegant job of setting the table, which means I kinda forgot about it, so if you'll get out the dishes, I'll open the wine for you and bring out the food."

"That sounds like a plan to me."

Quite frankly, if he could help Melinda Frye escape her abusive husband — and she'd known he would— it would mean a lot to her. Some cases just got to you. Chris Bailey was a force to be reckoned with, though she wasn't sure he realized how much he exuded that aura.

She knew her way around his kitchen and got out two plates and the requisite silverware as he uncorked the wine and poured her a glass. Outside, it was clearly late spring, with the tree frogs singing in chorus in the thickening dusk.

They ate sweet-and-sour chicken and pepper beef with stir-fried rice, and Anna sipped wine and felt some of the tension of the day ebb away. It didn't hurt to have a cute little dog curled up at her feet. She'd always wanted a pet but didn't have time for one. Neither did Chris, for that matter, but a kindly retired neighbor came over to let the moppet out during the day.

When he left for Virginia, she'd lose them both. His decision to accept a job with the FBI might spell the end of their tenuous relationship, depending on whether or not he was assigned back in Tennessee at the end of his time at Quantico. The moppet was slated to go to a couple in Ohio, who wanted her for the duration of his training.

Anna would just have to deal with it.

"So, here's a question." Chris rested his elbows on the table, his expression thoughtful. "Why would someone call me on my desk line and say, 'I know where his body is.'"

"No mention of a name?"

31

"No. He just said he'd be in touch, and I assume it's the same person who called back and left me, personally, a message. It said, 'Not six feet deep'. What's he doing?"

She thought it over; it felt disturbing. "I'd say challenging you in some way. Maybe taking you on to see if you can figure out who it is. Do you have any idea?"

"Of where the victim was killed, maybe. If it is the same victim."

"Oh, then maybe this person really is trying to best you in some macabre contest. You've gotten some press. There are people with strange obsessions out there."

"I was wondering about that myself." He sounded hesitant to admit it, looking away, his eyes shadowed. "Please tell me no one would ever kill a person because they want to taunt someone else."

"I will, if you will please tell me no one would ever beat the mother of his five children in front of them."

He looked back. "Okay, point taken. This is a big bad world. I get it. What does he want from me? Thoughts?"

"I think he admires you." She considered him from across the table, really weighing her answer, speaking slowly. "Maybe he wants to see if you're evenly matched. This might not be a new crime, have you considered that? Maybe he didn't even commit it."

"I have considered it, but the timing and lack of a body at what clearly looks like a crime scene makes me wonder."

"He might envy you." She toyed with her wineglass, thinking it over. Psychology was always interesting to her, that was why she'd studied it. "Perhaps you're really good at something he wanted to do and couldn't."

"That's an interesting interpretation."

"Without more to go on, it is hard to do anything but speculate, right?"

"I suppose so. So maybe he's a cop?"

"Or wanted to be one."

"Or a dangerous criminal. He's giving me clues." He got up and went to get another beer from the refrigerator in the kitchen, twisting off the cap as he sat again at the table. "It helps to think out loud, or at least it does for me. So, I know the gender of the victim and that it's a deep grave or a shallow one. That's not much to go on."

"There's a reason he's talking to you."

"I agree, and I don't like it."

"To me, that personal connection might be your key. At some point, he will make a pivotal comment."

"Will he?"

She thought so. "He's engaging you on purpose. There's something he wants to prove. You didn't find him, he approached you."

"Why?"

"I don't know."

"Yeah, me either."

Anna poured another glass of wine, gazing at him. "It's a contest. Or an old-fashioned walk down a dusty street with holstered guns. Who has the faster draw?"

"Shit, this better not be about me and the deadly shooting I did not initiate or want."

"I can't say, but my guess would be you've come to the attention of someone who's curious about which one of you, in a fair fight over the truth, would win."

"Well, so far I'm losing, but maybe it won't last." Chris looked unfazed. "Not to mention, I'm not alone. Carter is knee deep in this too. He's not a force to be discounted. Don't poke that bear, as they say."

"I'm pretty fond of Carter, actually."

Chris looked at her inquiringly. "You are?"

"He donates to the women's shelter, both his time and money."

He seemed surprised and then reflective. "I suppose that shouldn't stun me. That you take time there, and he does too. There's a story I don't know about him?"

"Yes, there is."

"But you do."

"No. I'm just agreeing with you."

"And you call me cryptic."

"What's fair is fair."

He raised his eyebrows. "Did I just win a battle?"

"Somewhat."

"Carter doesn't talk a lot about his feelings or his past."

"Well, neither do you." She gave a muffled laugh. "A match made in heaven?"

"We do disagree on many things, like an old married couple," he acquiesced, with a reluctant nod. "He thinks I shoot from the hip, and I think he doesn't draw fast enough."

Anna didn't disagree. "He's a good man."

"I'm in your camp on that."

"How are you going to solve this one?"

"We're playing a game of chess. My opponent's next move determines mine. Like you, I'm wondering if this could be a cold case and unrelated to our recent call. My problem is that he can freely communicate with me, but it isn't a two-way street. I have a number, but it is a burner phone, and there's no option to leave a message. I can have the location traced, but I have to have a serious case for that, and if the phone is turned off, can't do a thing anyway."

She considered it. "I think he'll be back in touch. He started this for a reason."

CHAPTER FIVE

I admit I challenged my enemy.

Hell yes, I did it on purpose. He had something I wanted and was not willing to let it go.

That he retaliated didn't surprise me at all. We were lucky to get all the horses out before the inferno became something that flared out of control.

My father looked at the ruins of that barn and set his mouth in a firm line I recognized. "They won't get away with this."

* * *

Three o'clock.

Ross was not getting much done, even though it was a busy day. At least he'd contacted a company and scheduled a tentative time for them to come clean the house, and, once the wiring was done and the electric back on, cart away anything left in the basement. That needed to be done anyway, and now more than ever.

The sheriff's department had cleared it, so that was one detail off his plate.

Ross was really hoping for this all to come together seamlessly and it had been going very well, but now the house was a potential murder scene.

Life tossed curve balls.

There had to be an explanation. He just wasn't positive he wanted to know what it was.

Cal walked into his office after a brief rap on the door. As he worked in the building next door, an impromptu visit was never a surprise.

"I just talked to the contractor. As soon as the plans are approved, we'll have the permits. So we're just waiting on Whitney."

"She seems on board."

"Did you really take her to dinner last night?"

So that was what this visit was about. Cal could easily have picked up the phone and asked the question. Ross said carefully, "I asked if she might want to have dinner with me and chose the Tanglewood to give her a sense that we really did look into this endeavor."

Cal sat down and looked at him directly. "Why is it I've always thought there might be an interest there?"

He replied, "Is there a problem if there is?"

There was a telling pause. "There is if the only thing you want is to get her into bed."

Considering Cal wasn't exactly an angel when it came to women, this was an interesting conversation to have, but it wasn't like Ross didn't understand that this was his friend's sister. "No worries, she's wary enough of me for both of you. What the hell did you tell her, anyway?"

"I didn't tell her anything. Men hit on her. Give her credit for having the good sense to weigh whether the interest is just sexual or if there's a potential relationship."

"I do, actually." Ross kept his voice mild. "I just know you and I have been friends for quite a while and hoped you hadn't shared any of our less-than-gentlemanly moments with your younger sister. Remember college? Lots of willing girls and lots of parties. We were not perfect."

That made Cal stop and laugh ruefully. "I get your point. Trust me, she hasn't heard those stories. I just sense she likes you and—"

36

"Want to make sure my intentions are honorable?"

"Something like that."

"Well, they aren't *dishonorable*, so relax. I took her to dinner. I didn't as much as touch her hand; there wasn't even a moonlit kiss."

"Honorable intentions and moonlit kisses?" Cal arched a dark blond eyebrow. "Are you reading romance novels in your spare time?"

"Oh, you bet. Unless there's football on television, then I might watch that instead."

"Good to know."

Ross gave him a level look. "I have no idea how she feels about me, but I just think she's attractive and intelligent."

"I agree she's intelligent, but — as someone who grew up with her — she's also sensitive. I don't think she takes relationships lightly."

"Point taken."

Discussion over. At least they were two reasonable men, or so he thought.

Don't hurt my sister. Message sent and received.

He wasn't sure on a possible involvement scale where he stood either, but he was interested enough to find out.

He changed the subject. "Did she give you a timeline?"

"She said by the end of the week. I gave her the original pictures from the historical society. She loved those old images."

"The faster the better."

"I agree." Cal looked somber. "I just wonder, since it looks like someone was maybe camping out there in the house illegally, if they're either the cause or the casualty."

"Good point. But we have no clue to as who, or even when, really. There hasn't been electricity in literally years. Luckily, the bank paid to have the plumbing lines drained so the pipes wouldn't burst, so there isn't any running water, either."

"I know, but those cans of food were put there recently."

"We should probably call the detective and tell him. Whitney mentioned that last night."

"On your date?"

Ross had to take a moment and sit back. "Does it bother you *that* much, that you keep bringing it up?"

To give him credit, Cal thought it over. "I don't know. I'm worried you might break her heart."

"Now who's been reading romance novels?"

"Okay, let me rephrase. I'm worried that with you, she's in over her head."

"Last I checked, I'm not a bad guy."

"I never said you were. When it comes to experience, she isn't a match for you. And romantic novels have nothing to do with it. I mean, she's the nice girl next door."

"I'm not the nice boy next door?"

Cal laughed. "Would *you* even describe yourself that way?"

"I suppose not. Would you describe *yourself* that way?"

"Probably not. But this isn't about me."

"Okay. Agreed."

"I'm just worried she'll fall for you and you won't commit. It seems to me as soon as any relationship you've ever been in gets serious, you walk away."

This was an argument Ross didn't expect this particular afternoon. "Isn't that the responsible thing to do? If you already know she isn't *the* one but start to get the vibe she thinks that about you, then you should break it off, rather than let it go too far."

"If we weren't talking about Whitney, I'd agree with you completely."

"I took her to dinner one time."

"Yeah." Cal looked skeptical.

"Can we switch back to talking about the hotel? She'll get us plans that quickly?"

At least the change in subject diverted the conversation again, or maybe Cal was willing to let it go. "She has a colleague that thinks it's an intriguing idea and wants to help out. He's older, and I want to say involved with the historical society in some way."

"That's a lucky break right there. We could use one at the Haunted Hotel." Ross smiled wryly. "I'm just throwing that idea out there."

"What about Spook's Inn?"

"That has a ring to it. Bloody Hand Retreat?"

"I kind of like that last one." Cal raised a brow. "May I point out we have no idea what happened?"

No, they didn't, but common sense pointed to nothing good. Ross suggested, "Since you're here, let's call Bailey and tell him we think there might have been an occupant. Maybe he'll want to try and get fingerprints from those cans we forgot to mention. I never thought of that, but then again, I'm not a detective."

* * *

William Beeson ran a finger along the seam of the picture and then pointed at the roofline. "Look at this. This is art."

Whitney agreed. "Can we keep the integrity of the design and give them what they want, so they can retain their designation as a historical building?"

"I believe so. I certainly hope so. This property used to be in my mother's family."

That was interesting. "Oh, I didn't realize that."

"It has quite a rich history."

"Ross Waylan and my brother will be delighted to hear that. There are investors, but is it going to be prohibitively expensive? This is my first restoration project."

"Material costs are up to the builders. We can adjust if need be, but that's really not our function. You know that."

She did. "This matters to people I care about, so I thought I'd ask."

"Your brother can figure the costs. I think it's a great project. That property needs to be preserved. I believe everyone would agree."

"I know *I* do. The house has good bones. Cal had it inspected and the foundation is solid, and no other real issues were found except general deterioration from sitting empty for so long, and the electrical isn't up to code. I can't believe with the age and location, there was very little termite damage, so the structure is sound. It's mostly brick, so that probably helped quite a lot."

"We can come up with the plans, but a consultation with an engineer will be necessary for a third floor."

"I agree completely."

He left for a meeting, and she went to work on the possible restructuring, though there was no doubt that there was a challenge in putting bathrooms in each room. Given the time period in which the house was constructed, the rooms were traditionally small.

Her phone rang, and she looked at the name with some trepidation.

What did Ross want?

"This is Whitney."

Of course he was amused; it was a stupid thing to say. "I realize that. I called you."

She wasn't sixteen, but he made her feel that way for some reason. "I'm at work, and always answer it that way when I'm at my desk."

He let it go. "We're having the house cleaned soon, so maybe you can actually go and get a better visual of the space and do measurements after that's done." Then he said dryly, "And maybe we could have dinner again, just so Cal can stop by and tell me how he doesn't trust I don't have evil intentions toward you. No, wait, *licentious* intentions. Better word."

There was no choice but to laugh. "Do you?"

"Oh, absolutely."

"Did he really do that?"

"My integrity is definitely in question when it comes to you. Oh, he has every right to be concerned, but still, it's a little insulting."

The banter was funny, but maybe it was just that. "Good to know about the house, and yes to dinner again sometime, especially if it will make my brother give you another lecture on proper behavior, since I'm fairly sure neither one of you are lily-white."

"I believe our quest was for just the opposite, back in college anyway."

"I'll let you know when we have the plans done. I started them this afternoon."

"I just wanted to know if you'll have dinner with me again." He seemed intent.

"How about my house? Tonight? We can discuss what one of the senior partners in the firm had to say. I think you'll be happy with it."

That was an impulsive decision, but she'd done it anyway.

He gave a low theatrical whistle. "That'll send Cal over the top. It's a date. I'll bring wine."

Why was it she thought maybe she was being naive? Then again, there was no harm in having dinner with an attractive man. She really hadn't met anyone in a while who interested her in the least. If there was one thing she knew about Ross, he wasn't boring.

Quite the opposite. He was charismatic in an understated way, that aura of compelling intelligence fascinating.

Smart and good-looking was tempting, but she was cautious. Her brother didn't need to worry about it. She was guarded about this all on her own.

On the other hand, was there any reason to sit home alone if there was another choice? Whether there was any chance of the relationship going further or not, she genuinely liked Ross. He'd never made a pass or said anything inappropriate — unlike more than a few of Cal's other friends. That probably underlaid his caution when it came to Ross.

She and her brother understood each other fairly well.

He knew she was tempted by Ross Waylan, and didn't agree necessarily.

Very well, but she was her own person.

"I'll see you around six thirty?"

"Sounds good to me." He responded and ended the call.

She'd make Italian chicken. That was easy enough to put together. Stop at the local bakery for some garlic bread, toss a salad, and there was an impromptu dinner.

"What are you smiling about?"

Whitney glanced up and saw that Ellen, one of the associates that did the financials for the firm, had paused in the doorway and was peering in curiously. "Aren't I allowed to be cheerful?"

"As a much older woman with daughters your age, I'm going to argue that's not 'cheerful', that's a *pleased* smile."

That was insightful, but not necessarily welcome. *Was* she pleased? Okay, maybe she was. She liked Ellen, so she supplied an answer. "Second date tonight."

"Cute guy? Of course he is. Look at you; why would you settle for anything less? *Nice* guy, now that's the real question."

"I think so. Smart guy, *that's* not in question. Polite and well-educated — and yes, he's good-looking. He might be a little too good-looking. I don't think he's spent a lot of Saturday nights alone, but I like him."

"Trustworthy?"

"I hope so. He and my brother are going into business together."

"I didn't mean it that way." Ellen smiled. "I certainly hope that works out, but I was talking about you."

"I have no idea about his previous relationships, but I guess we shall see what happens. It's just a date."

"Not a 'just a date' smile." Ellen shook her head. "Just an observation."

CHAPTER SIX

There was an old saying that resonated.
Everything in life comes full circle.
So it does.
Mine ended badly, but it doesn't always have to be that way.

* * *

Whitney lived in a small house just outside of town that she'd inherited from her grandmother, and since she didn't have to buy it, was able to renovate it very nicely, or so Ross had been told by Cal. He certainly agreed.

Whitney poured wine into two glasses and handed him one in a graceful movement. "I was the only granddaughter and was named after her. She left all the grandsons farm equipment and my grandfather's collection of antique stamps and coins, so, considering I had to really work on this place, we all probably broke even."

"Your grandmother was named Whitney?"

"Her mother's maiden name, so yes, she was."

It was a quintessential old farmhouse, but if she did half the job on their project that she did on this, he'd be happy. Polished floors, the finish on the cabinets matched the age of the house, and her taste in paint colors and furnishings really worked. She had pulled off something special: it was elegant yet comfortable.

"Did you study interior design too, or do you just have good taste?" He was sitting in a curved artist's chair at her kitchen counter, which had a base that resembled a splayed tree trunk with roots done in iron. He thought it was both distinct and just the kind of thing they needed.

"I did take some classes. As for good taste? Well, it's been dicey in men."

So this was how the evening was going to go?

That was fine. He preferred the teasing to her usual reserved approach. She looked great, too, casual in jeans and a short-sleeved silky pink top, maybe a hint of gloss on her lips.

"I have somewhat the same track record with women." He said it wryly, but also with honesty. "I might like what I see, but not what I get. Who knew I was sensitive enough to want to really enjoy their company, too?"

"Who knew?" She took a sip of wine.

He shot her a sardonic look.

"Just saying." Her return look was unrepentant with a hint of humor.

"Your opinion of my depth of character is duly noted. I think I'll change the subject. What did the partner in your firm have to say?"

"He thinks we can design it and keep the historic designation if we replicate the roofline for the third floor you want. He's on board with helping me, since I've never done this before, and he certainly is experienced on restoration projects. Not to mention — and maybe you'll find this as interesting as I did — that house used to be in his mother's family."

"Really?" That was added bonus, but maybe not a surprise. It wasn't unusual for generations of families to stay close. "Excellent."

He didn't just mean that news, but also the wine, which was smooth with a nice depth, and the view, which was of her moving around the kitchen, smooth hair shining, her profile delicate and very feminine as she checked the oven. He was a fan of all of it.

"I did call Detective Bailey this afternoon and left a message about someone maybe living there unknown to us."

"I think that was a good idea. Who knows if it means anything, but it could help if they saw or heard something."

"Or they're the injured party."

"That has occurred to me, too," she said somberly. "If you're desperate enough to occupy a vacant house with no electricity or running water, perhaps you don't know the finest people."

"I follow that logic myself." He settled back. "It has to be personal, whatever happened. Someone knew the occupant was there, or else they came there together. A bloodbath right inside the front door? There's nothing to steal, so that wasn't it."

"It doesn't look like it was an accident of any kind."

"I have to agree. When Cal called me, I wasn't even sure what we should do when it came to talking to the police. What? Say, 'There's some blood on my floor. Can you figure it out?'"

"I'm not positive the detective was even sure what to do, without any evidence an actual crime had been committed."

"But he came. I'd say a large pool of blood is evidence. Evidence of what is the question."

Whitney agreed. "I think we're all imagining the worst, but there was no body. Ugh, it sounds so gruesome to say that out loud."

Unfortunately, that was the first thing that came to mind. "There aren't really a whole lot of alternative scenarios, but we have to hope they *can* figure it out. Let me change the unpleasant subject. It smells great in here."

"And the wine is really nice."

"Thanks for inviting me." He meant it.

"You asked about having dinner again. I decided on home court advantage." Her expression was bland.

"Is this a contest?"

"Between men and women? Always, wouldn't you say?" She took a sip of wine, leaning against the counter in a casual pose, but she wasn't fooling him, because her remarkable turquoise eyes held a guarded look.

"It's always complicated, in my experience anyway. Just when I think I understand the opposite sex, I'm proven wrong."

"Maybe they aren't sure what you want, but I sense you're being self-deprecating."

"Okay, let me say I understand what they want, eventually, but don't anticipate it."

At least that made her laugh. "Fair enough."

"So just tell me. I'm open for that."

"Uhm, fairness, mutual consideration, and honesty."

"No memorable sex?"

"Okay, that too."

"Hopefully, I can provide all of the above."

"That sounds promising."

Definitely innuendo — he despised the word *flirtation*, since he wasn't in high school — but there was some mutual understanding.

She was different, but he didn't know how to define it. Quite unusual for a man who could close business deals with succinct, efficient language. Being at a loss as to how to express himself was not his thing.

So he said it plainly. "I'm not just playing around, I'm . . . interested."

"I just might be interested, too."

She wasn't shy; she was reserved. Whitney had poise and quiet confidence, and it drew him in. And if she was also on board with a possible romance, he was all for it. That surprised him even more.

They just gazed at each other.

Discussion over.

Dinner was delicious — he would eat that chicken dish every day, if he could — and they deliberately did not discuss anything serious, and that was relaxing, which he could use.

That, he was not good at. Relaxation. He was in his opinion very good at his job and at controlling his life, but he was not great at being laid-back.

Perhaps it was a balance between them.

Enlightening.

* * *

He helped clear the dishes, and afterward, he took advantage of the traditional walk to the door to turn and catch her by the waist and pull her close. The kiss was slow and provocative. He reined it in, because, while some women wanted it wild and fast, he had a feel for Whitney that she wanted the opposite. She was soft and supple in his arms, and felt amazingly erotic, even with the restraint.

Definitely not his usual style, but that was fine.

"Thanks for dinner," he whispered against her lips.

"My pleasure."

"No, mine." Then he let her go and stepped back. There were limits; he didn't want to pass her comfort zone.

Ross walked to his car, wondering at the wisdom of becoming involved with the architect on the project, much less his partner's — and good friend's — sister.

* * *

Chris got out of his truck and decided that it was not a waste of his time.

The old Ivy Manor was not unvisited.

Someone was inside.

He could see the dim light through one of the windows. It wasn't supposed to be there, he knew that. No vehicle out front, so whoever was there had walked, or perhaps ridden a bicycle and taken it inside.

A vagrant maybe, or even some local kids using the place for a hangout?

But if those phone calls were related to this . . . who knew? Either way, someone was trespassing, unless it was one of the two new owners of the property. He doubted it. Two apparently affluent young men — they were planning on financing a hotel project — would not voluntarily spend the night in a deserted old house, even if they owned it. The question was . . . who would?

He was certainly curious.

Only one way to find out. First, he went back to his car to get his flashlight and to call Carter. "Just wanted you to know I'm at the old Ivy place, and there's a light upstairs. Ross Waylan called me late afternoon and left a message. He told me they'd found cans of food in the house when they looked it over, and one room was pretty clean, so they wondered if someone had been squatting. I thought maybe I'd swing by. It looks like they might be right."

"Be careful. We may not know what it was yet, but something happened there."

"Don't worry. Big abandoned house, lots of blood, someone there that isn't supposed to be . . . I've seen a horror movie or two. I called you to let you know where I was just in case."

"Good idea. I'll know where to look if you don't show up for work tomorrow, maverick. Here's an idea: call for a deputy for backup."

"I'm thinking it over."

Chris ended the call and wondered just how smart it was to walk in that door alone or if he *should* call for a deputy.

The dim light went out.

He wondered if whoever was in there had heard him pull up or seen the arc of his headlights. Once before he'd had someone come rushing out of what should have been an uninhabited building; that encounter had ended in a deadly confrontation. He had no desire for a repeat performance. They knew where he was if they had as much as glanced out the window, and yet he had no idea where they were. That was a big house.

In the pitch dark with just his flashlight, he'd be an easy target.

He could come back tomorrow, when it was light, and look it over then — discretion being the better part of valor, or however that saying went.

The downside of that was, whoever was in there might change location if they realized he knew they were there, and he would lose any chance to ask questions.

Well, when he decided on this career, he knew some danger would be involved. Another saying came to mind: *Nothing ventured, nothing gained.*

He went up the dicey steps, braved the creaking porch and tried the door. It was locked, but just jiggling the handle did the trick. It was thoroughly rusted, which explained the easy entry for anyone interested in coming inside.

The big place was silent as a tomb. Dark, dusty, blood still on the floor, the metallic smell evocative of whatever had happened and of years of neglect. It was hard to tell if there were new footprints with just a scarce survey, because not only had police officers walked through this front door but the owners as well. And, of course, he was less than positive that entering now was the best course of action.

"Detective Bailey with the sheriff's office." He said it as calmly as possible, but loudly. "I'm not here about anything in particular, but can I talk to you?"

Not a rustle of sound.

That deep silence was both enigmatic and discomforting, since he knew someone was there. Whether they could hear or not was in question, because it was truly a large house.

"Police officer."

He skirted the drying mess and swept his light across the big room, gradually moving toward the back of the house. Huge empty dining room, with an elaborate chandelier hung with cobwebs, that would actually probably make a nice small intimate restaurant — a good fit for the intended upscale hotel, a step above a bed and breakfast with a historical feel, which was what he understood to be the intention of the new owners. Hardly his area of expertise, but it seemed like the place might be suited for it. There was a state park close by and several large lakes, not to mention rivers for canoeing and hiking trails.

Still silence.

The kitchen was dated but comparable to the rest of the house and he looked in the cabinets. After a few empty, dusty searches, he did find the promised cache of canned food and an opener, some wrapped plastic utensils and paper plates.

It seemed there was someone living there. It wouldn't be his choice, but it was shelter, anyway. Though he was fairly sure the new owners might frown on the arrangement.

He was undecided if it was worth it to fingerprint the cans. Unless the person living here illegally was in the system, it wouldn't be helpful and would just spend tax dollars for nothing. And who knew if they had anything to do with the blood in the entryway?

Though he'd really like to hear their take on what happened or might have happened.

Looking for more evidence he found it in the form of a small cooler tucked into a corner with two ice packs and some deli ham, mayo, and a loaf of bread.

Plus a sippy cup and a small container of milk.

Oh shit. Seriously?

He stood there, contemplating his options. This was literally casting around in the dark. There was a child involved? Chris just stood there, completely adrift on how to deal with this complication. He replaced the lid, stepped back, and decided to leave it alone until morning. This changed everything.

He went outside and called Anna. "I'm sorry it's late and I left, but here's the situation. The old house . . . someone's living here, and there's a child involved. They're hiding from me. I don't blame them because the words 'police officer' send people running, and they're breaking the law just by being here without permission, but I'm kind of at a loss."

"No electricity and no water?"

"Yeah."

"I'll be there."

"Anna, no. I didn't call you for Search and Rescue, I called because I need your advice on how to maybe coax them to talk to me — tomorrow, because tonight I'm just going to leave. Either I scared someone who is innocent or someone who is guilty, but put a child in the mix, a young one, and I am not doing this in the dark. Should I leave a note?"

"Okay. I get it. Let me think for a second." There was a pause. "I don't want them in that house by themselves — it could be a crime scene."

"Oh, you're talking to someone who agrees one hundred per cent, but they're hiding, it's pitch dark, and I also don't want them to have to stay in a closet all night. Help me out."

"Leave your number and say 'call me if you want help'. Add mine if you don't mind."

"Sounds good."

He went out to his car and got out a piece of paper from his notebook, wrote the note, and took it back, setting it in the cooler on top of the milk.

Enough for one night. Even he got tired occasionally.

He was headed to his cabin.

There was no question he needed to sit and think.

"Can I help you, mister?"

The voice came out of the shadows as he was walking back to his truck. Chris started, since he didn't expect it. A male voice, not precisely aggressive, but with an edge.

"Detective Bailey," he corrected in a firm tone, his hand going to his weapon as he turned, wary and extremely aware he was in uncharted territory.

"Oh." The young man stepped out of the woods near the drive and raised his hands in a supplicant manner. "Sorry. I just wondered why you were here. This property has been empty for quite some time. I live as next door as it gets to this place, I guess, since my house is kind of far away. I saw someone had pulled in."

That was of interest. "How often do you see that?"

"Well . . . it caught my attention. It seemed like an odd time to be showing the house to someone."

"I'm not a buyer."

"I get that now. It must be the badge and the holstered weapon. Are you a fed?"

Chris never answered questions, and he'd already identified himself. He didn't dress in uniform, by any means, and never wanted to again. "And you are?"

There was a slight hesitation. "Frank Williams."

"Mr Williams, how often do people show up here? Have you noticed a lot of activity?"

He seemed to consider it. "No. I know the place finally went on the market, but not much really happened."

"But it sold."

"I thought it might have. The sign has been gone forever, so hard to tell."

"No one coming and going since then?"

The young man shook his head. "But I don't watch over the place. I play video games at night, or watch television, you know."

Fair enough. He'd been watching tonight, however, and it was getting late.

That was of notice.

"I'd appreciate a call if you do see anything unusual." He took out a card and handed it over.

"Will do."

CHAPTER SEVEN

The short and the long of it, as my father used to say, just came to a difference of opinion.

He was a wise man, short in stature but long in wisdom, and I was saddened to lose him.

Especially since it was my fault.

So was my mother, for he was the love of her life, and she wasn't the same after he died.

Guilt is hard to live with, I discovered.

Some things just go that way. The mistakes I made definitely had consequences.

I realized I would lose the love of my life, and I did.

Or perhaps she lost me.

* * *

The figures looked good.

Construction costs were high, but they could swing it and the timeline was reasonable.

Perfect.

Whitney's initial outlines looked good to him, but Cal was about construction management, not design.

But not all was going to plan.

The sheriff's office had asked for them to stay having the remediation company come in and put the builder on hold for a few days. He had no idea what was going on. Detective Bailey merely said there might be things that needed to be settled first.

What the hell that meant, he wasn't sure. But the delay was annoying, and the fact that no one seemed to be inclined to tell them exactly why was frustrating.

Cal called Ross. "Beer? I'm buying."

"Of course. Invite Whitney? I take it this is a business meeting."

"Or you want to see Whitney. Just a guess."

"Could be. Or she's part of this, so she should be included." The tone was neutral.

That was true.

"Name the place."

"Lil's?"

"I'll pick up Whitney if she can make it. Or you can call her."

He was being somewhat obsessive about this, Cal had to admit it. "I'll call, and you pick her up. Deal?"

"Good."

End of call.

End of story? He wasn't sure. They were both adults, and at the end of the day, it wasn't his business. Whitney was a grown woman. If it was her choice to pursue a relationship he thought might be a gamble, he needed to keep it to himself unless she asked his opinion.

And she hadn't.

Her silence bothered him the most. She didn't *want* his opinion. To him that meant she'd already made up her mind. That was fine. Ross was a great guy — if he chose to commit.

If.

He called Whitney. "Drinks on me, and a confab on the house? Ross will pick you up."

"I can do that."

"I think the three of us have a date, then."

"I'll see you later."

They met at a small bar he liked. Lil was still the actual proprietor, and she waited tables. She had an ample figure and a friendly smile, and she remembered everyone.

"Hotshot. Good to see you." She plunked down a beer and took a seat. "How's your dad?"

They'd gone to high school together, so she always asked about his father. "He's good," Cal told her. "Holding his own as always."

"I'm glad. Always liked Bill. He and your mom are nice folks. They come in for a bite now and then."

He absolutely thought the same thing. His parents were nice people. Both he and Whitney were lucky in that regard. "I won't argue that. And here comes my sister and my friend." He made a wry face. "Or maybe more her friend now, it's hard to tell. I'm paying tonight, by the way, so give me the bill. A glass of white wine for the lady, and Ross will just have what I'm having."

Lil gave Ross a once-over glance as they approached. "She sure could do worse in my opinion."

Most females seemed to feel the same, in Cal's experience. "Yeah, I'm fine with it if he's sincere."

"Don't ever sell Whitney short. She's damn smart for such a pretty girl. I'll get your drinks."

It was interesting to see them walk to the table. Ross's hand was at her waist, and that familiar and possessive gesture meant something.

She's with me.

Whitney did seem to be noticed when she walked into a room, and they at least looked good together.

Maybe it would be fine.

Cal was skeptical but willing to be convinced. He got politely to his feet because he was a boy from Tennessee. Some things you learned early on from a reasonable — that had been established already — but strict father.

"I ordered drinks," he said by way of greeting. "Whitney, I just said white wine, so you're victim to Lil's decision on that one, and Ross, you get whatever lager she brought me."

"Sounds fine." Ross pulled out a chair for Whitney and then sat opposite when she sank down. "I take it this really is a business meeting, and you weren't just longing for my company."

"Well, I have figures for construction costs and thought we should all talk it over and discuss money and any options we might have. It takes all three of us to make this discussion worth our while."

Lil arrived with their drinks and whisked off after giving Whitney a meaningful smile and a wink of approval over Ross, which Cal had to admit was obvious but funny.

He handed them each a sheet of paper. "Here we go. Let's see what we can come up with."

Ross was about the money, Cal was about the timeline and difficulty of the project, and Whitney weighed in on if they could accomplish it or not.

She took a delicate sip from her wineglass and thought about it. "To put in the bathrooms, we need more space. So we have a wall to extend, and we have to replace the roof anyway, so let's keep the existing structure, but just add more? I think I can do that, and the plumbing can go in there, but it will affect the symmetry of the house. So, for the sake of appearance, do it on both sides? Can you find old brick?"

This was why he wanted this meeting. "I believe I can."

"At a reasonable price?" That was Ross, and why they were talking to each other on neutral ground.

"I think so. There's an old bank being torn down; maybe if we offer to take it away, we could just have it. Very close to the same period."

"Okay. I see the purpose of this conversation."

"How close in time?" That was Whitney, intent and practical.

"Turn of the twentieth century, so not as old, but it looks like it would match fairly well."

"That should work. I'll check with the historical society."

The conversation continued in that vein, and he was glad he'd suggested this, so they could talk together instead of just relaying information back and forth. A unified vision was what he wanted, since this had been his idea ever since he spotted the listing for the property.

They all walked out together. It was odd to watch Whitney and Ross get into the same car.

His mixed feelings were his problem and he knew it. This was either going to work out really well or very badly.

* * *

Whitney was just amused; there was no other word for it. "What do I not know that has my brother so worried?"

They were at her house; Ross was about to drop her off, and she'd invited him in for a drink.

"If I had to call it," Ross said, "he wanted this project, but recognizes none of us have done anything like this before, and it makes him nervous."

She leaned against the counter. "Are you?"

"No. It's solid and will make money."

He sounded confident, and that was her summary of the situation as well.

"He's worried about something else."

"Like you and me?" Ross was serious, those dark eyes direct. "He thinks all I want is to get you into bed, and then I'll walk away. He was pretty straightforward about it. Is that what you think?"

He asked in such a forthright way, she took a moment to answer.

"No." She didn't, and it wasn't going to work like that, anyway. "He needs to give us both more credit than that. I don't do casual sex."

His smile was wry. "Don't get me wrong: you, me, and a bed sounds great, but I'm not looking for a transient relationship either."

"Nice to know we're on the same page."

They just looked at each other, and whatever Cal thought, she believed Ross. After all, they'd only shared two dinners and one kiss. It wasn't like he was giving her the hardcourt press. Even better, he was willing to discuss it.

"So what's next?" The question was asked with a slight twitch of a smile. "The lady's choice."

"Maybe have dinner again?"

"My pleasure. Tonight?" He lifted his brows.

"Three nights in a row? Cal won't approve." She had to laugh.

"I'll risk it."

"Just don't tell him. He's not the keeper of my private life, though I appreciate he cares."

"Of course he does. I have a sister, and I suspect I would be protective as well if he was interested."

"The weaker sex and all?"

He shook his head and a lock of dark hair curled over his forehead. "Weaker? I think I'd argue you all have the upper hand most of the time."

"Good to know. What do you have in mind?"

"Order a pizza?"

She wasn't in the mood to cook, so that sounded fine. "After having a refined and very businesslike meeting at a classy establishment like Lil's, how can we possibly eat take-out pizza?"

"I know. We should fly to Paris and dine at an exclusive restaurant to counterbalance, but I think pizza right here and this cold beer would be fine with me."

"A down-home boy at heart?"

"Just hanging out with the girl next door."

"What?"

"Cal's words, not mine." Ross looked genuinely amused. "Hey, it's a compliment. He just was saying you're a nice girl. I agree, you are."

"I'd prefer 'woman', if you don't mind." She regarded him over the rim of her glass. "I don't think I've been a girl for a while."

"Every inch a woman. Don't think I haven't noticed." The rejoinder was smooth and his gaze deliberately appraising.

"I think you're being lascivious again."

She was going to sleep with him. Maybe not tonight, but it was such an odd feeling of inevitability. He knew it too. It was there in his eyes.

"Anything is possible."

"You chose the word."

She did like his sense of humor. And other things about him too, which was the problem.

"Only because my initial choice was not accurate at all. No evil intentions, quite the opposite."

"Glad to hear it."

"Let me demonstrate." He set aside his beer and got up to walk over. She placed her glass of wine on the counter because she knew what he was going to do. It wasn't like she was unwilling when he pulled her into his arms and kissed her with a lot less restraint than he'd shown before. Not just mouth to mouth but body to body — what he wanted was not exactly a secret.

Cal might be right warning her off. Ross was dangerous. Tempting? Well, yes. But if he was just playing around, she wasn't his type.

"I don't—"

"Do casual sex, I'm aware." His mouth brushed hers again and he let her go. "We're both on a learning curve here. Do you want me to order the pizza?"

His hands eased from her waist and it was over, though she wasn't going to forget that kiss for a long time. "That sounds fine," she said, letting her hands linger on his shoulders just for a moment.

He noticed.

So did she.

If he was a mistake, she was going to make it.

* * *

If it wasn't for the call, he might have actually gone to bed and slept. "This is Bailey."

59

"Good evening, Detective."

Smooth drawl, sophisticated delivery. He went on full alert. "I got your last message."

"Of course you did. Doreen is a nice woman. Very efficient."

He knew her name. Interesting, though it was hardly a state secret; she was the contact for the county sheriff's department.

Chris said, "What are we discussing this time?"

"The murder was intentional, but motivated by something even you will never guess."

Well, shit.

"What murder?"

Of course, the person hung up.

Chris just looked at his phone. What the hell was this game, anyway? This time, the person had called his cell.

He knew them? No, he didn't recognize the voice, except from the previous call. They knew *him.*

Adversaries? He was starting to think this person was truly testing him. Anna was right.

It was the keywords "even you". Naturally, he called Carter, even though it was pretty late. "So, third contact now. Who can you think of that I've pissed off?"

"Besides me?" Carter was predictably sarcastic. "Have you ever even glanced at a clock?"

"Not often enough. I'm being serious here."

"What did he say?"

"I don't like he mentioned Doreen by name. He also said she was a nice woman and efficient. My question is whether he knows her, or it was just an observation from talking to her for less than a minute."

His partner took that seriously. Carter's tone altered. "No, I don't like it either."

"He said the murder was intentional, but I would never figure out why."

"What murder?"

"Good question."

Silence. Finally Carter muttered, "I'm thinking about this."

"Is the caller someone we know?"

"Someone we know who's underestimated you. Like I said, I'm thinking."

That was pretty close to being a compliment, and Carter didn't do them often. Or ever.

"I just don't get the game quite yet." Chris was thinking too.

"Cat and mouse, except why he's taunting you in particular escapes me."

"You and me both."

"There's a link. We just don't see it. We should sleep on it and talk at a more reasonable time."

Cold cases. He needed to circle around and check those out in the database again. *Something I'll never guess?* What the hell did that mean? He sat back and rubbed his forehead, because occasionally, he got just plain tired. Not often enough, but it happened.

Carter might be right. Some sleep might be in order.

Not an option.

He wrote down: *New crime or old one? Location of the body is significant to the caller. Motive is also an issue. Who, why, and where?*

He didn't really have a clue. Literally.

It didn't help that the moppet gave a gentle snore at his feet. At least *someone* was sleeping.

He signed in and pressed a key and started to look again.

CHAPTER EIGHT

It was a long story, not told, but played out in short phrases; there was no give or take.

The contest was useless, as there would not be a winner and they knew it.

Yet they fought the futile battle anyway. Both sides suffered losses, and the rancor increased as the stakes grew higher and there was no end in sight.

I likened it to some of the medieval conflicts I'd read about in school. Down to the last man standing.

Only I was the first fallen.

* * *

Malice Aforethought.

Ross sat at his desk and thought it over.

It was a book written in 1913 about a murder on an estate in Tennessee. Why did he have the uneasy feeling it might be pertinent? It had arrived in the regular mail. He'd opened it curiously, seen the faded cover and discerned the age of the book, and wondered why anyone would ever send it to him.

No note, no anything.

Then he suspected exactly why he'd received this particular gift.

The house they'd just purchased was the scene of a horrific crime just before the turn of the century? A brutal murder that led to a small deadly war between two families.

Great.

As a businessman, he was hardly thrilled with that news, but as a person, he was more concerned with why anyone would bother to send him the book in the first place. Recent events, too, lent it a sinister — he couldn't come up with a better word — slant.

Whitney's associate with ties to the historical society might be able to help with it.

A good excuse to call her. He'd wanted to do that anyway.

She answered briskly with just her name, but her tone softened when she realized who was calling. "I'm sorry. I didn't realize it was you."

"No problem; you're at work. This question relates not only to our project but to the man you work with, the one you consulted with about the house, who has ties to it. Didn't you say he was a member of the historical society?"

"Will Beeson? Yes, he is."

"I think I might need to talk to him. Possible?"

"I'm sure it is, but I can do it if you like." She sounded understandably curious.

He hardly blamed her for that. "This would be a show-and-tell conversation," he explained. "There's been an interesting development. I should probably call Detective Bailey as well. I'm kind of at a loss as to how to take it."

"I . . . see. Well, let me rephrase. It's hard to say without more information, but I'll ask Will if he has time available, and maybe you fill me in on it later?"

"Another evening together? I'm all for that." He meant it, too, which was unsettling. There was no denying he was interested, but was he serious? That hadn't happened yet in his life, so it wasn't like he could define just how he felt. In lust, oh hell yes, but that wasn't exactly the poetry in motion of a romantic relationship. Was wanting someone on a sexual level the same as wanting to spend every free moment with them?

He could be walking a fine line he'd never balanced before.

"How about meet at the house later?" she suggested. "I could get a better look and do some measurements."

If he hadn't gotten a request from Detective Bailey to stay away until further notice, that would have been an absolute yes. "Not tonight. I think there's more to what's going on than we know. That's why I want to talk to your colleague."

"Oh."

"But a definite yes to filling you in." The moment he said it he gave an internal rueful laugh. "Okay, that sounded all wrong. Sorry, I swear I wasn't being suggestive. I meant if you want me to explain, I'm more than happy to tell you over a civilized glass of whatever beverage you might want, in a polite setting."

She laughed. "That sounds fine with me. My house, then?"

"That sounds like a date to me."

It did, actually. Were they dating? It seemed like they were. It sounded better if he thought of it as *seeing each other*. *Dating* sounded far too much like two college kids. They were both past that.

He amended. "I'm all for it."

"Me too. Seven o'clock? I'm really interested. Oh, that sounded suggestive, too."

It was his turn to laugh. "This new development might draw your attention."

"How so? Now I'm intrigued."

"Let's just say the house might be more historical than we think, but not necessarily in a good way. You'll have to wait for it with a glass in hand."

"Really? Fine, Mr. Master of Suspense, I prefer Chardonnay or a nice Merlot."

"Ask and you shall receive. I'll bring both. See you then."

The call ended and he went back to his current dilemma. The picture on the cover of the book was a blurred, very old photograph of what appeared to be the house, obviously taken a very long time ago, a huge oak tree near the front veranda that had been taken out by either Mother Nature, time, or the hand of man, because it wasn't there now. The porch that had replaced it was in bad shape, so it had been gone for a while. *If* it was the same house. It certainly looked like it, but probably could be any southern mansion — but why else would anyone send it to him?

Was this worth sharing with the county sheriff's department? Someone sent him a book. Hardly a crime.

He didn't know. Maybe Whitney could weigh in, or Cal might have an opinion.

He was at work and had things to do, but he had to crack it open and at least look.

The opening was chilling.

I opened the door not knowing who stood on the other side, and my worst enemy had a knife. I knew it was going to end badly but I had always known it was going to go this way. Hatred is very powerful and we both had it in measure.

Ross didn't have time to sit and read a book in his office, but he had to admit he was riveted. He didn't recognize the author's name, but a quick search should clear that up, and surely if this pertained to their house, there would be information out there.

Who was Richard Gothard? He'd never heard of him.

Written in first person? He was hardly sure how to take this whole thing, but it was strange and disturbing. Was this Gothard connected to the family who owned the house so long ago?

What he really needed was to get back to the business at hand. His schedule was already full.

This could be addressed later.

Or maybe not.

His phone pinged and he didn't recognize the number. The text message just said: *Did you get my gift? Happy reading, though it isn't a cheerful story.*

In consternation, he stared at it and decided maybe later wasn't a good idea.

* * *

He was late, but she was not exactly on time either. There were plenty of projects in the works without the one Whitney was taking on freelance for Cal and Ross, and she was scrambling a bit. That was fine. Too busy was better than not having enough work, so she had the feeling with this ambitious new endeavor Ross was in same situation.

She was just making a simple spaghetti sauce and had stopped and bought garlic bread and packaged salad.

Ross did arrive bringing two bottles of wine, so that was good. He had also brought something else.

"Smells great in here." He handed her the package. "What do you make of this?"

She slid a book out of the envelope, examined the cover, and looked at him incredulously. "What is this?"

He opened the wine and poured it into two glasses. "I don't have a clue as to what it is, but I'm going to venture a guess: since someone was murdered in the house long ago, somehow this is a message. What kind of message? I'm not sure. If you can enlighten me, I'd appreciate it."

There was a picture of the house on the cover and the book itself was obviously old. She looked up at him. "Someone sent this to you?"

"And sent me a text asking if I received their 'gift'." He leaned against the counter, still in tailored slacks, but he'd lost the tie and unbuttoned the top of his shirt so he looked like a poster boy for company casual, stylish but relaxed. Except the set of his shoulders told her he wasn't all that at ease. Attractive? Oh yes. Relaxed? No.

Not that she blamed him. "That's bizarre, and not in a good way."

"Tell me about it." He exhaled audibly. "So now what do I do? First we call the sheriff's office to report a puddle of blood and then we tell them someone sent me a book? If I were them, I would be concerned not at all. No crime has been committed, that we are aware of."

A valid point, she had to admit. "I don't know. That was more than a puddle, and that hand print was disturbing."

"If you want disturbing, read the first few paragraphs of the book."

What she wanted was a nice glass of wine and a calm evening, but evidently that was not going to happen. This was *disquieting*.

"Written in the first person," she reflected out loud after she read the first page, "but published so long ago the author is gone."

"I would guess. So is the publishing house, so there's no one to ask. I looked for it online. The historical society is my best recourse, I suspect."

"This is why you want to talk to Will." She shook her head, setting the volume aside. "I get it now. He might be able to steer you to someone who knows about this or could research it. I guess my main question is, why send it to you?"

"That is a very good question, isn't it? I don't know. The motivation completely escapes me. If it's just to give some insight into the history of the house, that's fine, but why not include a note? The anonymous part bothers me."

It did her as well.

He looked at the book, which she'd set on the counter, and lifted a brow. "My inclination is to just not bother anyone with this. I don't know what they're even supposed to do. No harm, no foul. They have more pressing issues, I'm sure."

She could see he wouldn't want to be calling in inconsequential reports too often. But in her mind, and obviously his as well, something happened in that house recently — and now there was this hint at a past crime?

"I don't know what the point of it is. I admit I'm puzzled."

"Then we both are."

"I'd consider this cautiously."

Maybe about more than what they were discussing. There was wariness between them that spoke volumes about how their relationship was evolving. The house/hotel project aside, they needed to figure out a personal balance. She thought it was working so far, but there was a reason the saying "don't mix business with pleasure" existed.

He read her too easily and raised a brow again. "You're extremely cautious. I've noticed that."

Subject changed.

This was so awkward, and yet inevitable. Carefully, she said, "Just so you know, I literally have no idea what I'm doing if we get more involved."

Well put, she thought.

It took him a moment — maybe it was the look on her face or the way she said it. But she saw him straighten from his pose against the counter. "Are you saying what I think you're saying?"

She blushed, or at least she could feel the heat in her face. "I don't know. What do you think I'm saying?"

"Whitney . . . you're being serious?"

She took a sip of wine. He'd chosen well; it was nice and smooth with a deep resonance in the body, but not too fruity. She liked it. "You and I have already had this discussion. I can't even imagine casual sex."

"I guess you really are the girl next door."

She just looked at him. "Sex seems like a very intimate thing to do with someone you don't have deep feelings for."

"As beautiful as you are, I can't believe . . ." He just stopped talking. Which was a nice compliment, so she had no idea what to say either.

For some reason she felt embarrassed, like she'd admitted she'd never learned to swim or ride a bike. "Thank you, but it's my choice. I just walk away if I feel it isn't more than superficial interest."

His smile was charming but rueful. "This is ironic, but I had that discussion with your brother. Not exactly the same topic, but he pointed out I'd never had a really serious relationship, and I replied that if I knew it was not going to work, but they started to get the wrong idea, I cut it off. It seemed like the right thing to do."

Waiting for each other? she wondered. Then again, maybe that was just a romantic notion she should get out of her head.

"I try to listen to my inner voice, and if it says 'don't do it', then I try to pay attention." She took her wine to the counter and sat on one of the stools. "If we're getting introspective here."

"I think we're having quite a conversation."

"Apparently, in some ways, we are like-minded, then."

"Not a bad thing, considering the context of the discussion."

"Let's switch it back to this." She pointed at the book.

"Let's hope it isn't a copycat crime that left that bloodstain." His expression was somber.

"I wondered about that as well, but why would someone do that?"

"I don't have a clue. How did they even find that book, or know Cal and I bought the house? The whole thing is strange, and I don't like any of it. Why did Detective Bailey essentially ask us to stay away?"

"I don't understand it, either." She didn't. All of a sudden this project had thrown her life into disorder. "He didn't say?"

"He seems to be a man of few words."

"You fall into that category as well."

"I do?" He looked genuinely surprised.

"He didn't say why, and you didn't ask him, either."

There was a hint of acknowledgement in his smile. "I tend to defer to law enforcement, though I'm happy to say I don't have a lot of experience. Cal and I might have gotten into a dicey situation or two in college, where we might have been drunk in public walking home from the bars or a frat party. Otherwise, law-abiding citizens."

"I have to wonder if Cal got a similar message."

"You think this is about the hotel?"

Did she? "I don't have the slightest idea, but your purchase of the property seems to have caught someone's attention."

He propped his elbows on the polished counter, his glass balanced in his hand. "I don't disagree. What to do now is the problem."

CHAPTER NINE

It was so questionable whether I'd brought it on myself.

The jury was out.

Maybe I had.

Dislike is such a tangible entity. Once it introduces itself into the room, it refuses to leave. I disliked my enemy immediately when it stepped in, like a bitter taste in my mouth, and he knew it.

It is quite obvious in the end; he felt the same way.

His fiancée didn't share his aversion to me at all.

* * *

Warm azure skies fading to dusk.

No visible movement. It was ostensibly just a big, empty, decaying house, the epitome of shabby elegance.

Anna got out of the car and closed the door with a gentle push. "I have no idea what we're walking into, but to be honest, like you, I never know exactly until I'm in the moment."

Chris said with emphasis, "If you think I'd let you do this alone, you'd be wrong."

"When she called, she didn't want me to tell you. I convinced her you were a nice man as best as I could."

He gave her a look of reproof. "Anna, I'm not here to arrest whoever this person is. I'm here to ask her if she knows what happened. That's it. So far the owners haven't even filed a complaint. I couldn't arrest her if I wanted to, at least for trespassing. All she'd have to do is tell me she had permission, and I would have to prove otherwise. I know she doesn't, but the law is the law."

"She called me, so she wants help. Don't interfere with my job, and I won't interfere with yours. Let me talk. Deal?" Anna was adamant about this and knew he'd comply but wanted to be completely clear. That cautious phone call had spoken volumes to her.

"Absolutely." He stood there, tall in the slanting sunlight, but luckily, he always looked casual. He was intense, but it didn't show most of the time.

"Let's go see what we've got."

The door opened easily enough. Chris insisted on being first, yet he let her be the one to call out. "Loretta? This is Ms. Hernandez. I'm so glad you called me. Can we talk?"

"We can."

Hushed voice from the shadows. She'd been waiting for their arrival. That was a good sign. The woman was standing at the edge of the room, wary, but at least there. She did have a child in her arms. Two years old at the most. Anna was a pretty accurate judge of age, given her profession.

"This is Detective Bailey. All he wants is to listen to our conversation."

"Ma'am." That was all Chris said, keeping his word.

"This is Chloe. You said you won't take her from me."

It wasn't like Anna hadn't faced this before. Her reply was succinct. "My job is to keep her with you, unless you're abusive or she's neglected. If neither of those things are the case, you're just fine. But what I *can* do is find you help so you have running water and available medical care if necessary and help to make sure she gets food and clothing. More importantly, to both of us, that she's *safe*."

"I want that, too."

Oh God, this woman was so afraid. Anna could feel it like ants crawling across her skin. "You're hiding, I get that. Let's go someplace safe with lights, food, anything you need, where we can sit and talk about how to resolve the problem. I promise you Detective Bailey will see us safely there. Your choice of location, but a dark house that belongs to someone else is not a good place to live. We can do better."

"Not a shelter. He'll find us there."

"Who is 'he'?" Chris was quiet and calm, but it was a good question.

She just shook her head.

"I have a badge." He pointed at his shirt. "And I also have a weapon. I will keep you as safe as I can."

Her response was both enlightening and telling. "So does he."

"What?" Chris looked sincerely unhappy at the idea of a dirty cop.

Anna said, with all the authority she could summon, "Let's go talk somewhere safe. Has little Chloe had supper yet?"

* * *

He had to admire how the whole thing was handled, but Anna was good at what she did.

Chris was stuck with trying to process the information without actually interviewing the woman. She obviously did not want to talk to him — that wasn't so unusual — but she also seemed frightened.

Anna was also very good at comfort food. She made French toast and fried some bacon, and the child ate like she hadn't in some time. For that matter her mother ate with enthusiasm, too, so neither one had eaten lately.

The darker side of his job followed him around all the time. Actually, he wasn't positive there was a lighter side on some days.

He had to admit that very young children were out of his scope of experience. At least to the extent that he'd never

73

had one come up to him, sticky fingers and all, and lift her arms.

Anna correctly read his expression. "She wants you to pick her up."

What?

They were at his house — Anna's decision, not his, but he supposed it made sense. If you were avoiding someone in law enforcement, go stay with someone else who could defend the fort. At least he'd had some bread and eggs on hand, which was why Anna had whipped up the breakfast-for-dinner meal.

He gingerly picked up the toddler, and she settled on his lap. The level of trust was appreciated. It could be because the moppet was nestled at his feet. If the dog approved of him, then perhaps the child did too?

What he *was* sure of was that he had some questions for the child's mother. "Tell me what happened."

She was young; he would guess just over twenty maybe. Distrustful of authority, but he wasn't a uniformed officer knocking on the window of her car. Instead they were in his house, and her child was in his arms.

"I don't know." The response was choked. "Kyle got involved with something. Suddenly he had money and then one night he said we had to leave our apartment right away. I grabbed Chloe, assuming he meant a motel somewhere, but he brought us to the abandoned house."

"Can I have a time frame?"

"About two weeks ago."

"You'd been there that long without running water?" That was Anna, her tone moderate and sympathetic.

Loretta nodded. "There's a hand pump out back that works. The water is cold, but it is water."

"How did he find that place? Did he say?" Chris was trying to tie it all together.

"He said it was empty and we'd be safe. That's all I know."

He looked at Anna in a silent plea for help. Thank goodness, she delivered. She had at one time been married to an attorney, so she understood how to ask questions. "I think Detective Bailey needs to know if you can get in touch with Kyle. Or if you can't, any information on the police officer you think might be involved."

"I haven't seen Kyle since I found the blood on the floor."

Of course, she started to softly cry, and it wasn't like Chris blamed her. Two possibilities came to his mind. He killed someone, so he was on the run and afraid to answer his phone — or someone killed him.

Either way, he wanted to find out.

"You didn't hear anything?"

"In that house, I heard noises all the time. In the dark, alone except for Chloe. I had this lantern thing he bought for us, for when the sun went down so I could at least read her a story or something. I watched some shows on my phone."

She hadn't answered his question. It happened all the time, so he was used to guiding people back to the topic at hand.

"Was he there that night? Did someone knock on the door, or was there a reason he went downstairs, like an unusual disturbance?"

"I don't know. He just never came back."

That man's child was sitting on his lap, and her mother was just so young. At not quite thirty-three, he felt the edge of experience. "This little girl is in the middle of this. Tell us all you can."

She made a helpless gesture with her hand, swiping at her damp cheeks with the other, her lips trembling. "All I know is that whatever they were doing couldn't have been legal, or he would have told me. I had the feeling he just didn't want me to ask, so I didn't."

"Is Kyle a police officer?"

"Oh, no." She shook her head. "No."

Considering all he did was ask questions, any ostrich mentality escaped him. He tended to look directly at problems. That made it easier to deal with his job, but there was

75

a part of him that understood not everyone approached life that way. "What makes you think a law enforcement officer is involved?"

"Kyle told me not to worry, that he was *working* with someone with a badge and a gun."

Great. An echo of his own words. That was disturbing. "But no name?"

She shook her head. "No."

Still casting around in the dark. "Has his family heard from him?"

"I don't know. They don't like me because we got pregnant, so I can't talk to them."

"They will talk to me." Chris said it decisively, and he meant it. "I assume you at least know where they live."

"Yes."

At least a place to start. He needed that. "I'd appreciate the address."

She nodded unhappily.

"I can arrange for a safe place for you and Chloe to stay," Anna said, "but for now you can stay here. You'll be protected, and Detective Bailey can figure out the rest of it tomorrow."

At his house? Well, he guessed it wasn't the first time he'd offered refuge, but he certainly wasn't prepared in any way for a toddler.

As usual, Anna had it handled. "I have a folding crib in my car. I'll stay as well. Is that okay? I bet your daughter would like a warm bath. Do you want to do that?"

"Yes." Barely a whisper. "I so would."

"Let me show you the way."

He watched them go up the stairs. This was one of the more interesting evenings of his life. Beer went with French toast, right? Chris got up and took one out of the refrigerator and sat back at the table.

When Anna came down, she said unapologetically, "You have an extra room, and they need safe haven."

He was amused more than anything, except also impressed with how she'd arranged it. "Did I say anything?"

"I just commandeered your house." She defiantly swept a lock of dark hair behind her ear.

"Yes, I noticed that. It's fine."

"You don't mind?"

"I don't." He really didn't. Not if she was going to be there as well.

"Thank you."

In exasperation, he said, "Anna, we are playing on the same team. If I can help, I will. Don't thank me."

"Chloe is a fan."

"Tall man with a gun. I was a little surprised."

Her expression said it all. "Never sell children short. They can tell good guys from bad guys, usually."

"I wish I could." It was a dark observation. "I really can't stand the idea of someone who's supposed to protect and preserve the safety of the public betraying that trust. It casts a shadow over all of us."

"Kyle is dead, isn't he?" Anna's voice was very quiet.

"That would be my guess, though I'm not supposed to operate under any assumptions, just consider the facts at hand."

One assumption he was making was that whoever had been calling him knew Kyle. So the blood on the floor, the missing young man, and connection with law enforcement was starting to at least form a tentative link.

Or there could be no connection at all. In any case, he needed to address Chloe's missing father and what might have happened to him. "I'll find him."

Anna had made a cup of coffee. She cradled the mug in her hands, her expression resigned. "I'm afraid you will."

He was afraid of the same thing. *Not six feet deep.* "Either to arrest him, or find out what happened to him."

"In my experience — and I'm sorry that I have any — people who are desperate enough to choose to put their child and girlfriend in a deserted house without electricity or water can't count on their parents, so that lead is probably a dead end."

He knew exactly what she was talking about. "I need a place to start," he said with an equal weight of wisdom. "I'm not counting on anything, but sometimes you catch a break."

"I know we need answers, but not sure I want them."

"A young father that's either a criminal or a victim. Sometimes I just can't win."

"Either one of us. Take children from an abusive father, but also take them from their loving mother, because she won't leave him? This isn't a contest between us, but realize I understand your point."

"Not perfect."

"Definitely not." Anna didn't dissemble, but then she never did. The forthright approach might not appeal to everyone, but he liked it.

"Where will they go?"

"Loretta and Chloe? I'll find out tomorrow. I just have to keep them safe."

"I would tell you they're welcome to stay here, but I have an uneasy feeling I might be part of this."

"What? How?" She stared at him.

"Some strange phone calls. It feels like I'm a target for someone. I just don't know why or who, but I think they know me through the job. Carter thinks the same thing."

"Badge and a gun?" She caught on quickly.

"I'm wondering. Just because you say you're a cop doesn't mean you are one."

She frowned. "So it could be anyone following the news that knows your name."

That summed it up. "It doesn't really narrow the field, does it?"

CHAPTER TEN

The choice was hers in theory, but the argument belonged to them. That was the issue at hand. Winner take all.

It was hardly that simple.

Neither of us understood it.

Walt Whitman wrote in Leaves of Grass, *"Putting myself here and now to the ambush'd womb of the shadows." Not being much of a philosopher, I'm not sure what the poet meant, but I related to the sentiment. Born of the darkness rather than the light, that was my fate.*

I read that book many times.

* * *

The office was adorned with maps, pictures, and hand drawings on the paneled walls, and the desk was quite impressive and definitely antique.

Historical guy, Ross told himself. Maybe he'd come to the right place. Older and distinguished, William Beeson greeted him affably and shook his hand like an old-fashioned gentleman. "Whitney's friend. Nice to meet you. Good choice. She's a winner all the way around. Brains and beauty."

The assumption his interest was sexual was hardly inaccurate, but that everyone just went in that direction was disconcerting. "She does have both of those attributes going for her. She thought you might be able to help me gather information about the property because you have a connection to it."

"I can do my best, since I've already looked into it."

That was convenient. He could thank Whitney for that. "I appreciate your time."

"I think you'll be fascinated, or at least I was. Did you know that it was built before the Civil War by the Maddox family, and they used it as a hospital at one time? During the cholera epidemic, I believe. That was later. The son of Robert Maddox was a doctor, and he insisted."

That was nice backstory for the hotel; he was aware of the bare bones of it.

"I recognize the name. I actually have a book outlining some of the early history."

"Ah, do you? *Malice Aforethought*?" His brows went up. "Very rare. How did you find that?"

"It found me via an anonymous donor. I haven't read more than a few pages yet."

"Really? How interesting. Well, in quick summary, Robert Maddox was a major landholder around here and chose to build that extravagant house, which, in my opinion, will make an excellent hotel. He named it Ivy Manor, after his wife."

That was good to hear about the hotel idea, especially from a senior partner in a prominent local firm. Ross's own parents had raised their eyebrows over the idea — that is, until he begun to get interested investors. "We are certainly hoping it will work out to be a popular spot, because the location is great. What else can you tell me about the house?"

"Well, this is Tennessee, after all. The Maddox family did have a feud with their neighbors, the Wheatleys. I think it lasted through several generations, and finally there was a classic argument over a woman that went bad. A Wheatley murdered Maddox's grandson because they were in competition for the same girl, and all hell broke loose. The neighbor paid a deadly visit."

Blood in the foyer? Ross hoped the walls weren't really bleeding.

"Let me guess, is it supposed to be haunted?" He didn't believe in that sort of thing on an intellectual level, but life often surprised him.

Or maybe was it death.

"Of course." Beeson merely laughed. "Aren't all old houses where there's been a murder reputed to have restless spirits? That killing set off an unfortunate series of events, and retaliation and revenge set in. The families wiped each other out, basically, is my understanding."

"Wild West style?"

"Something like that. 'Backwoods warfare' maybe would be more accurate. No dusty streets and high noon, but more like shotguns and the dark of a humid night."

"That is pretty interesting history."

"We have several diaries, and of course, the documentation of the deaths from the confrontation. I think they add some character to a building that I am happy will be used again. It was designed by a man fairly famous at the time for his work in houses of that style. I can get you all that information."

"This is all valuable." He paused, wondering if it was even important, but curious just the same. "The murder that set it all off . . . do you know what happened?"

"I believe the grandson received a visit from the jealous neighbor, and was stabbed through the chest with a knife. They never found the body, but there was a witness. There was an article about the event, and I think we have a copy of it, since it set off such a series of events. Not the first deadly standoff between two families, by any means. I would guess you are familiar with Shakespeare."

"I am, thanks to some diligent English teachers, but this sounds more like the Hatfields and McCoys to me."

"I agree it was a similar situation and is obviously not unique." Beeson merely shook his head. "I'd prefer if we all got along in this world but am old enough to be resigned that it is never going to happen."

"I'm afraid I have to agree with you."

"Do you drink whiskey?" Beeson pointed at a very unique clock on the wall with a background that looked like the Acropolis. "It's five o'clock. Have a drink to celebrate your endeavor?"

"I am a native son. I do drink whiskey now and again."

"It just happens I have a bottle and some glasses here in my desk. By the way, I'd like to see that book someday, if you don't mind."

"Yes to the book and yes to the drink."

That's what they were doing when Whitney stopped in the doorway, her brows lifting a fraction at the sight of them sharing a companionable drink. "I didn't realize there was a party going on."

"You're invited." Ross got up immediately and offered his chair. "This meeting has been enlightening."

"Thanks, but I'm heading home. You can give me the details over dinner?"

He was getting in deep quickly, because the invitation made his day. "Just tell me what time."

After she left, Beeson looked at him with open male amusement. "I think you might be in trouble."

"That has occurred to me."

"When a young man looks at a woman a certain way, as my grandfather used to say, he's a goner."

"Let me guess: he was a wise man."

"When he said it to me, I was married not long after."

Was he that serious about Whitney? Not sure yet, but maybe it was a glimmer of light on the horizon. "Thank you for the information, and for a very smooth glass of whiskey. I appreciate both."

He walked out, thinking it all over. It was obvious he needed to talk to Detective Bailey and at least see if the fact that a murder had happened in the house before meant anything. But how it could be relevant completely escaped him, because that was a century ago. He was more concerned with what had happened there recently that required them to postpone starting work on the building.

Bailey was good at asking questions, but Ross had a few of his own.

He also needed to talk to Cal, but because of Whitney, he was wary. Still, he called him.

"The Mysterious Mansion has quite the past," he said. "Whitney hooked me up with a partner in her firm who does restoration work, and he's also a history buff, apparently."

"Hold on, I thought we decided on 'Haunted Hotel'? Or was it 'Demonic Destination'?"

"The official title is still up in the air. Anyway, we need to get together and talk about it. That house is packing some drama behind it."

"Okay, I'm intrigued."

"Call your sister. Ask her what she's fixing for dinner."

* * *

Cal stared at the phone in his hand. "Fuck."

Not very original, but applicable.

So yes, Whitney and Ross were seeing each other. It wasn't he didn't trust the judgment of either one, but they were really quite different. Both were driven, but in conflicting ways. Whether they'd ever understand each other was the question on his mind.

He did call his sister. "Okay . . . I just talked to Ross. Dinner a problem?"

"Well, no. I can handle it if you can accept in a gracious way that Ross and I are having dinner together again."

She certainly understood *him*.

"I don't want him to walk away from you." He had a valid argument.

"You know what? This is not your problem."

"That point taken, I'll be there for the table set for three . . . or can I bring a date?"

That silenced her for a moment. "What? You're seeing someone and not telling *me* about it?"

Guilty as charged. She was right; he was being intrusive, but his intentions were good anyway.

"Just answer the question."

"Oh no, please bring this date. I want to meet her. I'm just making spaghetti, salad, and garlic bread. There should be plenty."

"Done deal, if she's free."

"Can I be as critical of your choice as you are of mine?"

"Hey, Ross is one of my best friends, so I'm not being critical of him as a person, just worried for both of you if it doesn't work out. And you already know her."

"I do? Who is she?"

"We'll see you later."

"Cal!" she said in exasperation.

He pressed a button and ended the call, laughing to himself — but ruefully, since life was ironic. The next call he made was to Beth, asking if she was free for dinner this evening, and not telling her where they were going when she accepted. He was still at the office and it was past the time when he usually left, although he often took paperwork home with him anyway and caught up after hours.

The news about the house . . . he really was curious. What he thought they were doing was just buying a big old place and turning it into a hotel. It sounded good on paper. Ross could certainly handle the financial part and he could direct the remodel, but now what? Good news or bad news?

Either way, it was going to be an interesting evening.

* * *

The sauce did smell good, spicy with oregano and garlic, and Whitney knew Ross would bring wine.

Relaxing dinner? Whitney doubted it. Ross had some tale to tell if she knew Will Beeson, and she wasn't sure any of them wanted to hear it. And now, she had an unexpected guest.

If Cal was interested in someone, she was glad, but was he just as guilty as Ross of a lack of commitment?

As she moved to set the table — for four — she mentally sifted through who she knew that might interest her brother, and came up with a few possibilities, but no definite one that stood out. One of his former girlfriends she'd already met? Hard to say. Well, she'd find out soon enough. There were other issues to deal with, like bloody handprints and redoing an old house that might or might not be a crime scene.

Not to mention dealing with her own personal life.

Ross was the first one to arrive, and he had indeed brought wine, so that she didn't have to worry about having enough with the added guest.

She greeted him without preamble. "Do you know who Cal is dating?"

He lifted his brows. "I don't. He hasn't said anything."

"Well, we will soon."

He set the bottles on the counter. "Not to make us sound like simple creatures, but men don't ask about things like that. We tend to not talk about anything that personal. Don't ask me why, because I can't explain it. If your brother asked me if I love my mother, I might pass out from shock."

"Do you?"

"Of course I do. She gave birth to me and made me pancakes when I was little. I'm obligated to love her, but not eager to talk about it."

Whitney had to laugh. "That is one view on it."

"I'm just pointing out my male perspective." His mouth quirked into a smile.

He looked dangerously attractive, as usual, and she might not be as impervious as she thought originally; the resistance was waning every day. That magnetic smile alone was unforgettable.

"Thank you, by the way, for the interview with Beeson," Ross said. "He was very helpful. We didn't talk architecture, we talked history. He'd looked into it, and I'm divided on whether it will help or hurt our project, but I'm going to wait until Cal is here to tell the story. Should I open the wine?"

"That would be fine. I'll admit I'm wondering just what was said that led to two glasses of expensive bourbon."

"An interesting discussion of how people deal with conflict and each other."

"So you are being evasive?"

"No. I just want to tell the story one time. To you, your brother, *and* the mystery woman apparently. I see four place settings on the table."

"Yes, she's also going to be here, whoever she might be."

"He won't say?" He picked up the corkscrew she'd already set out and deftly went to work on the wine.

"He danced around the answer."

A few minutes later, she discovered why. The woman who walked in with her brother was more than familiar. They'd been college roommates, and before that, gone to high school together. Whitney couldn't have been more surprised. Elizabeth Garret was a quiet girl, hardly Cal's type, but Whitney had always wondered if she'd had a crush of sorts on him. Oh, she was pretty, with long brown hair and blue eyes, but definitely a wallflower. She never put herself out there.

Whitney couldn't quite picture it. Her brother and Beth? Well, maybe.

They were opposites, but so were she and Ross, as far as she could tell.

An interesting turn of events, but they were friends, so it was a welcome one. "Beth?"

"Whit." Tentative hug, but fine.

The dinner seemed to be met with approval all around, but it was hard to go wrong with pasta. It wasn't until they were done eating and the plates cleared that Cal asked bluntly, "So, what the hell? Just tell me about the house."

Ross looked contemplative. "It has a dark legacy. Murder and vengeance, along those lines. Of course, it is supposed to be haunted, which might be why no one wanted to buy it but us. From a business viewpoint, I think that might even help the hotel . . . except for recent developments."

"Like blood all over the floor?" Cal audibly exhaled. "Elaborate, please. Murder? Like what?"

"Some disagreement over a woman. It started a feud that ended with two families essentially wiped out, because it turned into a small private war. As I understand it, someone came calling and stabbed the grandson of the patriarch right there, and all hell broke loose."

That sounded grim, Whitney had to admit. "Will told you this?"

"Yes, he did. He's going to see if he can get the archival records for me."

"How long ago?" Beth asked in her understated way. "I work at the library, and we have several books on the history of this area. That surely would have been of note."

"Turn of the century. Not this one." Ross seemed interested. "Late eighteen hundreds. You work at the library? Who is Richard Gothard? Have you heard of him?"

"No. I'll look him up."

Whitney and Beth had been the unusual ones in their sorority in college: the architect student and the aspiring librarian. Neither career glamorous, but maybe it was why they liked each other. Neither one of them cared either about social stature or popularity, so they were friends because they were like-minded. Still, Whitney was trying to picture her brother with someone so reserved and wasn't positive it was a match, but it wasn't her decision. Cal was just as positive she and Ross weren't exactly a match either.

At this point, it was anyone's guess. Romance was never a sure thing.

"So, a bizarre copycat killing, patterned on something that happened a long time ago? And who's the victim?" She was just thinking out loud.

"Let's all keep in mind as far we know, there's not been a crime," Ross said. He was ever pragmatic. "If there was, though, Detective Bailey has information on that; I don't. I'm going to call him when I have more to tell him."

"I think you should." Whitney rested her elbows informally on the table. It was impossible to erase the sight of the bloody foyer from her mind. Something had happened there, and it hadn't been pleasant.

CHAPTER ELEVEN

I was like the first bullet being shot at Lexington.

Nothing but death and destruction ensued, and I own that at least some of it was my fault. I coveted another man's woman, but in my defense, she returned my feelings.

It was dangerous and foolish, yet irresistible.

Essentially, we made a death pact with each other, without realizing the fire that ignited it would cast a pall of smoke that would smother so many.

* * *

Loretta had cooperated and filed a missing person report on Kyle earlier that day — no time limit needed, because he had been missing more than long enough to start a search immediately. Which was how Chris found himself, with his partner, visiting Kyle's parents that evening.

Carter was good at this part of the job. He looked like a detective, and his inflection and choice of words were effective. "So you haven't seen or heard from your son? Please tell us the truth. Because, keep in mind, we are trying to help."

Mrs Sanders looked stricken, pale but silent. Her husband spoke for them both. A big man with stiff, broad shoulders, he sat in an offensive posture in an expensive leather armchair and didn't give an inch. "Who knows where our son might be? Kyle never has believed in rules, and if he got in trouble, I'm not surprised."

Chris told himself to stay out of it, but maybe he spent too much time with Anna, so he said it anyway. "Your grand-daughter doesn't have her father right now. She spent last night at my house because they had no place else to stay. All information is welcome. We need to find him."

"How is little Chloe?" Mrs Sanders finally spoke in a quavering voice. Middle-aged and just letting her hair go nat-urally gray, no make-up and dressed very plainly, she looked like a downtrodden wife. Chris had the feeling she just might be one.

"She's fine," he assured her. "Now in the care of some-one who will make sure she's provided for, but I heard her ask her mother twice where her daddy was. I have Anna Hernandez's card, if you would like to make contact with social services."

"No, we don't." Charles Sanders was curt and unrelent-ing. "And you're looking to the wrong people. We don't speak, so Kyle wouldn't turn to us. He isn't welcome here and he knows it."

When they walked out to the car in the darkening evening, Chris couldn't help but mutter, "Damn glad he wasn't my father."

Carter agreed, "I wish I'd never met a stubborn bastard like him before, but I have, and yes, you wouldn't have fared well with someone like him."

In unwilling amusement, Chris asked, "What is that supposed to mean?"

"You have a tendency to just play your hand and ignore the odds at times."

"I didn't impregnate a teenage girl, which seems to be Kyle's grave sin as far as I can tell. I agree that was preventa-ble, but he's hardly the first and won't be the last. Sometimes it only takes one reckless moment."

There was a pause, but then Carter said something personal, which he almost never did. "You're talking to a man whose oldest daughter was born six months after he got married."

The longer he worked with his partner, the more Carter took him by surprise. Day to day, they seemed to not see eye to eye on almost everything, but long term, they had the same goals and philosophy. He wasn't quite sure how to comment on that revelation, so he looked at Carter over the top of the car. "So, both you and I think his father is a judgmental asshole, and we have to choose another way to investigate this. We started in the right place, but no dice. Any ideas?"

"Kyle had to have had a vehicle. It wasn't parked at the house, so either he or the person who possibly killed him drove it away. Let's get the make and model from Loretta and hope he legally registered it. In any case, the apartment complex where they rented should have that information about the plate. We'll ask for it."

"That's a solid idea, for sure."

They got in and pulled away, and he called Anna, because Carter was driving as usual.

"Can we get some information from Loretta? Kyle's parents were just not helpful. We need to know the make and model of his car and the address of their apartment. With the formal report, we're now actively looking for him."

"I'll ask her and get right back to you."

"You took them back to my house, didn't you?"

"Of course I did. Loretta's so young, and she's justifiably terrified. I understand that she doesn't want to go to a shelter, but she's old enough I can't place her in foster care. I could put Chloe there, but there's no reason to do that I can see."

"Anna . . ."

"Aren't I talking to the man who offered *his* home to a potential murderer who had maybe wiped out his whole family?"

That he had to acknowledge, but she was talking about a previous case where he'd assumed responsibility for an underage boy accused of a crime he did not commit. "I never did think he was guilty. We don't know what we're dealing with here. What did Kyle get himself into? We have no idea."

"Why is it I believe there's no need to come after his girlfriend and child? She knows nothing."

"You and I realize that, but does whoever he's been dealing with know it?"

"I have no idea, but I refuse to put her into the system at this time. When you know more, let me handle it from there."

"I'll keep you informed, if you'll do the same."

Carter turned on the road back to the sheriff's offices, looking somewhat amused. "A decisive woman, huh?"

"Oh yes, she is. Ask her ex-husband. When she decided he was interested in another woman, she just filed for divorce. Not impulsive, just being practical."

"Sounds like it. What's she going to do when you leave for Virginia?" The normally businesslike Carter really was in a rare talkative mood this evening.

"Whatever she wants."

It was true. Chris was the one leaving, and he could hardly ask her to wait and see where he'd be assigned. That involved a commitment he wasn't sure he was willing to make yet. He'd never been in love with his previous girlfriend, Sara, but definitely had missed her when she'd left.

He gave up on dissecting his feelings to focus on the issues at hand. "So we pursue the lead on his vehicle?"

Carter agreed. "I can't see we have much more."

He couldn't either. "At least we have a place to start."

"Assuming Loretta describes the vehicle correctly, but I'm doubtful she'll know the license-plate number." Carter seemed skeptical. "My wife is an intelligent woman, but while she could tell you what kind of car I drive, I doubt she has the license number memorized."

It was true, men seemed to pay more attention to that sort of thing. "Well, if she just says it was a brown truck or something like that, we might be back to square one."

"What we have to face is that he wouldn't be the first man to abandon a woman and his child. If he suddenly had money and a chance to be free, maybe he just left."

"There is the issue of the blood and the handprint."

Carter was pragmatic as ever. "If he was into something illegal, those guys take each other out all the time."

That was one way to look at it, he supposed, but Chris still didn't like it.

* * *

At least she was able to do better than syrup and bread this evening. Anna made chicken and noodles from scratch, and green beans. She didn't have time to make them but picked up chocolate chip cookies from the bakery. Her companions seemed to love everything.

Both child and mother ate once again like they were starving. It was a reminder that the world was not a fair place.

Chris's arrival was met with both relief and apprehension, but he simply shook his head. "I don't have anything to tell you yet. It smells great in here."

He wasn't big on imparting information, so Anna wasn't all that surprised. "Did his parents at least talk to you?"

"They did."

"Have they heard from him?" Loretta asked it anxiously, looking so very young in worn jeans and a high school T-shirt with the emblem of a panther on the front. Anna had offered her use of the laundry room because there was no way a toddler could possibly have enough clean clothes after two weeks of no hot water. Loretta had gratefully accepted.

"If they had," he said quietly, "I would have told you, but his father made it clear they don't speak anyway, so my impression — and theirs — is he would not turn to them for help."

That was a long answer for him, so he was obviously aware of her fear and uncertainty, and at least sensitive to it.

Loretta said, with a quaver in her voice, "They were awful to him, or his dad was, anyway. At first I thought it was about me, but he said no, it had been that way all along. He could never get any approval, so he gave up. He wanted to go to college and he had the grades for it, but they wouldn't help him once they found out I was pregnant. He worked construction instead. I had to stay with Chloe. We just couldn't afford daycare." She added, "My mom is a single mother, and I have two younger brothers. She just can't do it."

Anna had heard similar stories often enough. "I can help with that."

Chris was no stranger to people in bad situations either. "Then listen to Ms. Hernandez. She knows exactly what she's doing. I'm sure Kyle would want you taken care of, wherever he might be right now."

That was, unfortunately, probably the only way to put it. Chris was, after all, a police officer, so he just spoke in truths. They didn't know where Kyle had gone, voluntarily or involuntarily.

"Okay." Loretta looked at her daughter, who was sitting on the floor next to the little dog, playing with a stuffed panda, her little face intent. Then she gazed at Anna directly, her expression poignant. "Whatever you can do."

A practical girl, given her age and situation.

Chris looked tired, and Anna wouldn't be surprised if he forgot about lunch half the time, so she made him a plate. "Cold beer?"

"What a great idea. I'll get it. You don't have to wait on me."

She caught the hint of amusement in his tone; he knew she was trying to make amends for inviting guests into his home without really asking him. But his was truly a safe house. Until Anna understood what she was dealing with, he was a necessary part of the equation.

Tall man with a gun. Exactly what the situation called for right now. Something bad had happened in that old house.

"I'll get it." Loretta got up and went to the refrigerator and brought back a bottle and deftly twisted off the cap. "I waited tables for a while, and yes, I'm underage, but I can open a bottle of beer. Some places aren't too picky about your age, as long as you'll do a good job and are willing to work, especially the late shifts."

"Well, thank you." Chris looked nonplussed for a moment. Her smile was tremulous. "No, thank you."

In Anna's assessment, Loretta was young but more worldly than she should be. It was probably why Chloe was a happy child. Her mother was aware enough to protect her, at least to a certain extent.

The toddler came over and bonked Chris on his knee with her stuffed toy. He laughed, which Anna guessed he hadn't done all day.

"I believe I can arrest you for assaulting a police officer, young lady." He grinned at her.

Naturally, she did it again, giggling right back.

"A repeat offender. When I finish my beer, I'm taking you in for sure."

He will make a great father someday.

Anna dismissed that wayward thought quickly, because their future was so uncertain it wasn't in the cards; she needed to be realistic. She wasn't even sure she'd ever commit again. So *never mind* seemed the best stance. But children trusted him. She did, too.

Not what she needed.

Detective Bailey was dangerous, she decided. An interesting blend of hard-to-read intelligence and compassion, coupled with a razor-sharp edginess.

"I'm fairly sure panda violence should be reprimanded." She put down her own plate of food and sat, so he didn't eat alone, which she suspected happened all too often. "Unless the culprit is really cute."

"Exactly." He smiled. "Cuteness gets them off the hook every time. It works in court. I guess I can arrest her, but why waste my time? I'd have to put on a tie to go testify, so not worth it."

Even Loretta laughed, which was much needed, at a guess. "Chloe, it's time for bed. Bring your bear."

When they left the room, Anna said quietly, "No luck, then?"

"Now that a report has been filed, we're really looking into it. Thank you for persuading her to do that. I can tell you, his parents never would have."

"No, that's my impression also. It's the father. He's some kind of religious zealot, and the pregnancy was not acceptable."

"Kyle's mother asked about Chloe's welfare. I agree, I'm not at all fond of that man. The real question is, where would Kyle turn if he was in trouble, since he can't go to them? We're casting around in the dark here."

"I'll ask Loretta if she has any idea. We've been talking."

The meal must have been good, since he ate every bite, but Anna always had the impression he was thinking about something else, and that eating was just a necessary interruption to his day. She'd never known anyone so focused.

Well, her ex-husband Trey had been somewhat the same, with a singular abstraction when he was working on a difficult case.

Her taste in men was questionable when it came to her personal emotional well-being. Her mother had pointed that out more than once.

"Any close friends? We need that sort of thing. That she didn't know much about his car wasn't helpful. Make and model is fine, but if they got it recently, he hasn't licensed it yet."

"She doesn't even have one now." Anna said, thinking out loud. "I need to fix that somehow. No transportation, no job. I don't like to create welfare moms. If Kyle left her voluntarily, she's going to be on her own. Even if he didn't, she's still on her own. The equation is pretty clear. If he was supporting them, he isn't any longer. She can't count on his parents to help, or apparently her mother. The first won't; the second can't."

He gave her a level look. "I try to solve crimes, not those sorts of problems. What are you going to do?"

She'd thought about it all her long day. "Maybe if she can get certified for CPR, see if she can get a job at a day-care? She does a good job with Chloe. That would solve two problems at once. I'm working on it. She isn't going back to working at a bar illegally if I can help it."

"I know a few guys that deal with used cars. Not saying they're all that savory, but they might be able to find four wheels that turn for a reasonable price. I'll ask."

"That sounds promising. She has virtually no money, but I have a few aces up my sleeve."

"I'll do my best, and at least it will be legal."

That was important to her, too. "Thank you for letting us stay here."

He finished his beer and set the empty bottle aside. "Anna, of course. But you owe me for subversive panda attacks by a two-year-old."

"What's the price?"

He raised his brows with a wicked grin. "I'm thinking it over."

His phone rang then. He looked at it, all humor fading away. "Let's see what my new friend has to say this time."

CHAPTER TWELVE

The house was silent and empty, like an abandoned stage after the play had ended and the theater had closed. Windows stared like dark eyes and there was no sound but the creak of the tree frogs.

It was a ghost now, a shadow, a backdrop for untold stories.

Mine included.

I wandered the halls often enough, not quite sure what I was looking for, but drawn in for some restless reason. The memories haunted me, and I could still hear that derisive laughter echoing like a refrain.

My childhood was a faint recollection so faded I resented the loss. I don't remember the touch of my mother's hand any longer, or the sound of my brothers' voices, or even the lonely sound of an owl hooting in the night, waiting for a response.

I'm adrift and aware of it. And I can't do anything to change it.

* * *

It was an unknown number, but he answered it because he was expecting a call.

Just not this one.

"Where are they?"

Ross was at his desk, and he leaned back in his chair, startled by the terse tone. "Excuse me?"

"You own the old Maddox property now, correct?"

"I do."

"Did you just throw them out?"

"Who?" *Oh shit.* "Wait a minute. Someone *was* living there?"

"Staying there temporarily. Tell me, what happened to them?"

"Who is this?"

"Someone very concerned for his girlfriend and kid."

This had to be one of the most interesting phone calls he'd ever gotten. Very evenly, he said, "I don't live in the house; I just own it now. We told the police we thought someone might be there, because we saw the food. I know nothing about a child. Here's a number to call, just give me a second to pull it up. Detective Chris Bailey might know something. I never saw them, so I can't help you. But no, we didn't throw them out."

He retrieved the number and carefully relayed it.

"Thank you."

The line went dead, and he just sat there, unsure what to do.

Then he called Cal and described what happened. The response was typical. "We knew it already. Any man who says 'thank you' might be okay, so let Detective Bailey deal with it."

"So someone was living there? How is that possible?"

"Just for a roof over their head? I'd point out the many drawbacks, like no water or electricity, but okay. Maybe someone would do it. Better than a tent in the woods, I guess. They called you?"

"There's evidently a child involved. I *am* letting Detective Bailey handle it, because I have no idea what to do."

"A child?"

"I'm afraid so. What the heck? We bought an old deserted house. I just thought it was a great business idea when you brought it up."

"We apparently bought a problem."

"Maybe. Or it was a brilliant move with unexpected complications."

Cal was an optimist, so he agreed, after a contemplative moment. "I'll roll with the latter. The house has history, so that's fine."

This idea might not be so brilliant after all.

Maybe Ross was an optimist, too. A possible murder in their house, most certainly many in the past, and he still had hope?

He did, actually. He thought the notorious stories behind the place would give it character. Recent events didn't necessarily help, but he wasn't convinced it would hurt, either.

"Yeah, that's a deal. Now, I guess I need to call the detective and give him a heads-up that I handed out his number to a stranger."

"I think that's a good idea. Keep me up to speed."

"Will do." He hung up and made the call.

It was an interesting conversation. "What? Who called you?" Bailey said. "This is important."

"I gave him your number."

"Did he say who he was?"

"No. And yes, I asked. He said 'someone concerned for his girlfriend and kid'. Why do I not have any idea what's going on?"

There was an audible exhale. "So he's alive. God, that's good news."

"Who's alive?"

"You gave him my number? That works, and I thank you for letting me know."

Not enlightened, Ross hung up and just sat there, thinking.

He did not have to be a genius to realize something had gone very wrong.

He's alive? What did that mean?

Whoever called him was very much alive. Angry at first, or maybe just afraid, and then calmer at the end. How did he even get the number to Ross's cell phone?

That was an interesting question.

He did the least logical thing and called Whitney. "I've had a weird afternoon. Am I being presumptuous or are we getting together this evening?"

"Presumptuous? I don't hear that every day." She was laughing.

"Yeah, well, your brother has already accused me of reading romance novels, so don't you start. It's a word."

"I read them."

"Romance novels? You're a woman. I'm a guy."

"I've noticed. Guys, for the record, are very interested in romance, in my experience."

He did have to laugh. "True enough. Not reading about someone else having it, necessarily, but I can't speak for my whole gender. Just answer the question. Do you want to have dinner with me?"

"Yes. What kind of 'weird' was your afternoon?"

"I'll tell you over some Mexican food."

"What girl can resist a margarita?"

"I'll order one for you."

"That sounds great, especially if you'll explain."

"I'll do my best, but I have no idea, really, what's going on. I'm standing on the sidelines, like a coach at a football game. I'm not really playing but trying to make decisions on where it's all headed. I would love to tell everyone what to do, but no one has handed me the information so I can come up with the strategy."

"Ross, you are so *you*. You'd like to direct everything, but that isn't always possible. I'll see you later."

Introspection wasn't his strong point. Maybe that was true.

If she accepted that about him, that was a positive. Didn't every man want a woman who understood him?

It had been a confusing day.

He didn't need this.

* * *

Whitney was in a particularly interesting place.

Unsure but yet . . . sure.

Ross did as he promised and ordered her a drink with one of those charming smiles the waitress seemed to appreciate. It arrived in all of its frozen glory, and she took an appreciative sip, then said, "Okay, Coach, give me the scoop."

"The problem is, I don't have it."

"What happened?"

He leaned his elbows on the table and just shook his head. "I got a strange phone call from a guy who wanted to know if I'd thrown his girlfriend and child out of the old house. I have to admit I was startled."

So was she. "That is somewhat unusual."

Ross smoothed his fingers over the side of his glass. "How could I answer an accusatory question like that, when we didn't know they were living there in the first place? I mean, we found the food and all, but I think both Cal and I imagined a toothless indigent who'd stayed a few nights, not a mother and child setting up house."

"What did you tell this person?"

"To call Detective Bailey. I gave out his number. The man didn't seem to mind. He actually seemed to know what was going on."

Dark evening and glowering sky outside, exotic music in the background, a good-looking man sitting right across from her and sharing their dinner. Things could be worse.

"So the legend of the Cursed Castle gets even more lurid?" Whitney gazed at him across the table, not particularly joking.

"There's a new name. I kind of like it. It has a ring to it."

"Tell me what he said."

"Bailey? It was clear he was glad the father of the child was still alive. What happened is still not clear."

"So this father was doing something associated with bad people?"

Ross looked at her. "I would guess."

That was chilling. "So where are they now?"

The overhead light caught his dark hair as he shook his head. "That I don't know. I didn't know they were there in the first place."

"In the Haunted Castle?"

"*Cursed* Castle."

She choked on her drink, hearing his ironic tone. "I keep mixing it up. There are so many possibilities."

"It isn't funny, I know, but Cal and I have been trying to pick a suitable nickname. It seems like there's been a lot of tragedy associated with that house, but hopefully, it doesn't include the last two residents. When we looked at it, it was empty, then we find out someone was living there."

It was difficult to imagine that. Lonely and dark and long-deserted. "With a child?"

"I know. I'd like to think I'm decidedly stalwart, but as a grown man, I'd probably be cowering in some corner."

"I know I would be spooked."

"I think there are a few ghosts maybe drifting around, if you believe in that sort of thing."

"I don't like being scared by something I can't logically explain." She was serious.

He laughed, but sobered immediately. "I can't say I disagree. I didn't get any details. Detective Bailey is a close-mouthed individual."

"He is that."

"So are we going to my house or yours for maybe an after-dinner conversation and a glass of wine, or something like that?" Ross tried to seem casual.

He knew she'd made up her mind. It wasn't there in his tone, but it was definitely evident in the way he looked at her. There was certain knowledge in his eyes that they'd crossed some line now.

She didn't think she was that transparent. Maybe he was just that perceptive.

"I think mine."

"Whatever you want. This is your call."

They were talking around what might happen next, and she appreciated he hadn't pressured her, because she'd been there before. She'd always walked away from that. In her opinion, he was courting her with an awareness of how she felt about it. This relationship felt different.

"Yes, my house."

"Fine with me."

They left the restaurant, his hand lightly at the small of her back. She recognized the play had shifted, and the ball was in his court. He knew a lot more about the game than she did. The real question was, did he just want to win, or was there more to it?

She knew she was going to have to take that leap of faith someday. No one else yet had seemed worth it, but Ross was pretty tempting.

It was more than just his physical appeal; she *liked* him. Good company, intelligent, a sense of humor . . .

At her house, she was about two steps inside before he caught her in his arms. It was a kiss with purpose, there wasn't much doubt of that — message sent and received. Not seductive but passionate.

He looked into her eyes. "I understand the word no perfectly well, but if it is yes, tell me."

She looked right back. "You already know it is yes."

"I hoped I was reading the signals correctly but had to hear it from you. I don't think any man should assume anything." His mouth teased the sensitive spot under her ear. "Bedroom and skip the drink?"

She was not necessarily apprehensive, but somewhat nervous about this decision. He knew it too, which was disconcerting. He murmured, "We aren't two teenagers fumbling around in the backseat of a car."

"I assume you realize I'm not on birth control." That needed to be said.

He smiled. "I considered that, due to a recent conversation, so no worries there. My responsibility. Upstairs?"

When she put her hand in his, she knew it was probably a life-changing decision.

And it was. She decided that in the aftermath, languid, being held in his arms.

Worth waiting for.

He'd made it that way.

CHAPTER THIRTEEN

One unreasonable party is all it takes for it to be a futile effort. All arguments have two sides. That I understand. Diplomats exist for a reason. Both sides need to see the equation, while weighing the implications of not coming to an agreement.

It is an overrated vocation.

They aren't going to do much good, in my experience. No one even tried, so the good old-fashioned argument was all that was on the table.

In simple words, there was only one way to right a wrong.

* * *

It was like something out of an old-fashioned spy novel, but Chris agreed to it anyway. Meeting at some seedy bar with stained tables and the smell of stale beer made him glad he carried a weapon and knew how to use it.

The badge probably didn't help, but it did explain, without words, the unconcealed gun.

A few patrons viewed him askance, but that was fine. He spotted his date for the evening without any problem, because the man's little daughter looked a lot like him, even at two years of age.

This was bound to be an interesting conversation.

He took a chair at the table. "I'm Bailey."

The young man across from him looked . . . hollow. That was the only way to describe it. Brown hair, a little long, the touch of a beard. Good-looking, yet just a bit unkempt, as if he hadn't slept much lately and pulled his clothes out of a backpack.

"Tell me about them," he said. "Are they okay?"

"Loretta and Chloe are fine. They've been staying at a safe place, thanks to a woman who deals with these situations very well. What happened?"

"I really want a beer. Is that all right?"

"I'll order one for each of us, since you're of age."

"You know that?"

"Kyle, I've met your parents, I know your girlfriend, and your child has sat on my lap. You and I aren't strangers."

"Oh, Jesus." He put his hand to his forehead. "And you're a cop."

"What did you do? One way or another, you're going to have to explain."

A passing server seemed to realize they were beverage-free and stopped. Chris ordered two lagers.

"Are you going to arrest me?"

"Can I? For what offense?"

"We were just moving weed. It was simple and didn't hurt anyone, and the money was good. Didn't raise it and didn't sell it. We just moved it."

"We?"

"A guy named Lattrell. I never knew his first name. He approached me. I wouldn't have ever done it, but I have a family to support, and they'd cut hours all around at my company. He worked there as a side job, part-time."

"Was he a cop?"

"He said he had a badge so he could get us out of being searched, and he sure carried."

That was not definitive information. No one named Lattrell worked for the sheriff's department, anyway. Maybe

107

another department somewhere, but there were no assurances the man had been telling the truth.

"I'm not DEA, so transporting marijuana doesn't matter all that much to me, especially if you aren't doing it any longer. I do care about a possible murder. Tell me what happened."

"I started getting threats."

"What kind of threats?"

"Against my life. Loretta doesn't have my last name and neither does Chloe, but they live with me. I was scared to death they might be targets too."

"Is that why you chose the deserted house?"

"Yes. Who would look there? It's big, too. There are places to hide."

Their drinks arrived then, so it stopped the conversation, but it was far from over. A pall of cigarette smoke hung in the air, but Chris tried to ignore it. At least the beer was decently cold. "A struggle for power?"

"I think that about covers it."

Sheriff Lawrence was going to love that, Chris thought darkly. A small drug war? "Whose blood was that? It obviously wasn't yours."

"What are you talking about?" Kyle Sanders stared at him.

"You never saw the blood? When did you leave the house?"

At least it would give him a timeline, if there had been a murder.

"I didn't decide to stay away. I had a long run. Lattrell didn't show and I had to go alone. I'm done with it anyway." There was panic in his eyes. "But they are safe, right? Ross Waylan swore to me they weren't thrown out, I just don't know where they are."

"They're safe. How did you find Waylan?"

The reassurance seemed to work, but Sanders took a decent swig from his beer before he answered in an uneven voice. "I gave Loretta my phone, but I have my laptop. You can find out just about anything you want if you know how. The neighbor, Frank Williams, was able to tell me the property had sold. He sort of caught me puling in one day and I said I was looking at it."

That was of note. *Williams lied to him*. Chris thought it over, and there was no choice but to wonder why.

"Where's Lattrell?"

"You tell me. I haven't heard from him. Maybe he was getting threats too." Kyle took a drink and then gave Chris a level look. "No, I didn't kill anyone. I can tell that's what you're thinking. A guy doing something dishonest, mixed up with the wrong people — suspect number one, right? I didn't. I only left Loretta and Chloe there because I felt they were better off away from me until I figured out how to get out of this. I couldn't call, because I left Loretta my phone but told her not use it unless she had to, in case they could trace it."

It was probably not a bad plan for someone who'd gotten in over his head. Chris said with patience, "Law enforcement is in place for a reason. Someone to turn to for help if you need it. Ever thought of that?"

"I was breaking the law. You weren't an option, to my mind. Besides, not every single one of you is a decent guy, for that matter." He added, "But you seem to be."

"I'd like to think so."

"If Chloe thinks so, that's proof. She's a tough sell. Like me, she does not like my dad. She'd never sit on his lap. Feel flattered."

"I did. I still do." She was a cute kid.

"What next? I go to jail?"

"I don't think so, but let's be clear . . . you've stopped transporting said illegal goods?"

"Yes." He was definite.

"Let's not overload our justice system, then. But please cooperate with this investigation."

"I will, but I don't know anything else."

"Let's go talk to the sheriff himself. Lawrence is going to be interested, and I could give him a report, but I bet he'd like to talk to you directly."

The young man didn't look too thrilled with the idea. "What if he doesn't agree with you about not charging me? I can't tell you how worried I am about Loretta and my daughter."

"They're being taken care of, and he's a reasonable man. Help him, and he'll listen carefully and maybe solve your problem. He's straightforward, so treat him the same way. Be up front. Never dodge a question."

"All right." Kyle was young, but he seemed to be in tune with real life. "If he doesn't agree with you, I suppose I deserve it."

"He's interested in the bigger fish. You can make up for whatever you did wrong by making it easier for him to do his job."

"Can I see them first?"

"Loretta and Chloe? Sure. We can go there right now, if you want."

The response was fervent. "I want that more than you know."

* * *

For a man of the law, he didn't actually play by the rules.

Maybe that was the attraction.

"He's going to stay here?" Anna was making dinner when they arrived. It had been priceless to see the reaction of both Loretta and little Chloe when both men walked in. Still, she was dubious if it was a good idea.

Chris had helped clear the table after the meal, and they both sat back down. "You know Carter would be happy to tell you that I make some questionable decisions now and then, but I think this is a good call. If Kyle is a bad guy, why were they both so glad to see him? Chloe has good instincts."

Kyle and Loretta were putting Chloe to bed — together. That child needed two loving parents. All children should have that, in her opinion.

So she couldn't disagree. "People do some questionable things when they're desperate. For example, no woman would ever choose to be a prostitute, yet it's the oldest profession in the world."

"Good point. And for the record, Vice would be the last thing I would want to work in in a big city, or even in a small one." He grimaced. "It always strikes me how we live in such a world of really good people like you, and yet there are animals prowling out there, just looking for anyone with a weakness, so they can take advantage of it."

"You reunite parents and children as well, or you did tonight."

He folded his hands on the table. "I think it comes down to not having much choice when he went to the wrong side. Now, I need to find out how it came about that he was presented that choice. Maybe he'll talk to you. He's completely worried about being arrested, and I suppose we could do that, but why? I know how to deal with bad guys; I just need to know who they are."

"Give me a ship and a star to steer her by?"

"Something like that."

"How dangerous are they?"

He considered it. "Hard to say. A lot of money could be at stake. I think someone was killed in that house, so if murder is on the table, pretty unpredictable."

"So you brought him here?"

"He needed to see the woman he loves, and his child. I'll stay up all night. I do that half the time anyway."

Anna gazed at him. "So the country boy detective is a romantic, huh?"

"You should know how romantic I can be, Ms. Hernandez." His mouth curved into a smile.

"I didn't mean in bed, but at heart."

He leaned back with a slight shrug. "I feel some empathy for him. He's young, and he's made some mistakes, but don't we all? He seems to own up to them, though, and I believed him when he said he wanted to see his family more than anything."

111

"I'm happy to hear that." She was, and she also trusted Chris's instincts. "If you think he's gone back to the straight and narrow."

"You'll have to pardon my language, but I think this has all scared the shit out of him." He added, "I'm giving him a pass if he'll talk to Lawrence directly. He's already given me one name that I hopefully can track down. He's all we've got right now, but after talking to him, I think this is bigger than one unexplained bloodstain in an old house."

"If so, then I'm glad you are a night owl."

"I guess there are some advantages to it." His response was dry. "I think I do more work sitting alone in the dark than I ever do at my desk. It helps me figure things out."

Anna could confirm that she'd woken alone enough times and come downstairs to find him scribbling notes, with his computer screen up and books scattered around him. "I've seen it in action."

"Besides, how could they possibly trace him here? These are ruthless people, but probably not sophisticated in general. It's probably just local. I don't think they'd cross that line."

"Because you're a law enforcement officer?"

"Yes."

"Oh, I get it. Because they know you aren't afraid to use your weapon."

She got a very direct look from those remarkable blue eyes. "We carry a gun for a reason. There aren't just choir-boys out there."

"Oh, I get that."

"Anna, I know you deal with angry people all the time." His tone softened. "All I'm saying is I'll be here like I'm sup-posed to be, between that doorway and whoever might try to walk through it to do harm to anyone inside."

Oh, God help her, she might be falling for him despite her determination to ignore her feelings. Yes, they were sleep-ing together, but that wasn't the same. Physical chemistry was great, but you could walk away from that. Emotional connection was entirely different.

She was once bitten and twice shy.

Loretta and Kyle came downstairs then, and it was touching to see them holding hands like high school sweethearts, though they had just put their child to bed and were hiding from people with bad intentions. Kyle won her over when he said quietly, "I got to read her a story. Thank you."

Maybe he was twenty-one years old, but not much more. In Anna's opinion, he had good self-possession for someone his age and in his position. "You can thank Detective Bailey. This is his house."

"Oh yeah, and that's my manly dog." Chris pointed at the little puddle of fur on the floor. "Life throws you curveballs now and then. But then again, she's been my only friend on more than one occasion."

"She's pretty cool actually. Chloe asked us to tell the puppy goodnight." Kyle seemed to meet with her approval too, since she let him pet her on the head. "So now what?"

"We'll meet with Lawrence in the morning, after a hopefully quiet evening." Chris sounded calm, his usual collected self, but with that edge of authority people recognized.

"And then?"

Good question. Anna wondered about that herself.

"It depends on whether or not we can determine who's been threatening you."

"As long as Loretta and Chloe are safe." He ran a hand through his hair and said raggedly, "This is so my fault."

Choosing to do something he'd known was against the law, yes, that was his fault, but it was a sliding scale. He did the wrong thing, but for the right reason.

Anna understood. "Help the sheriff's department, and in turn, I think I can help you get back on your feet."

CHAPTER FOURTEEN

Instability was a predictable trait in some families, like poisoned wine running through their veins instead of blood. Couldn't be trusted and heaven help you if you turned your back. I knew better than to do that, but always being on guard is wearing, and our dispute not something we could resolve.

I feared ever.

I was right.

* * *

He'd spent a satisfying night in the arms of a beautiful woman. It was admittedly challenging, because if she'd waited so long, he wanted to make it memorable for her — in a good way. Ross was fairly sure he'd succeeded.

He'd remember it always.

Life was full of enlightening experiences.

Like the moment his phone rang. "This is Anna Hernandez from social services. Is this Ross Waylan?"

It took a moment for him to run through reasons why anyone with social services would call him and didn't come up with one. He had no children, and his parents were healthy and well-to-do. "Uhm, yes. How can I help you?"

"I wanted to talk to you about your property. I have some clients that were occupying it who would like permission to go back and retrieve personal items."

He couldn't help it. "*Now* they're asking permission?"

"Yes." Short and sweet. "They were seeking refuge in what they believed to be an abandoned house. Now they realize it belongs to someone, so they're asking. Please give them credit."

That sounded fair enough to him. "Of course."

"Thank you. She's twenty and her child is two years old, so I appreciate it."

"They stayed there alone?" He sat there, not precisely in shock since he understood such things happened, but at least set back.

"When someone has very little choice, they tend to overlook the small things like no electricity or water or heat. Some people live in cardboard boxes on inner-city streets and alleys."

He understood how homeless people lived — but that big house, sitting so isolated and with nothing to offer but a roof and walls? He was horrified to a certain extent. "Are they okay now?"

"We're working on it, thanks to Detective Bailey. That's how I got your number."

"He and I have been handing over each other's numbers, so that's fair enough. I think I talked to that child's father."

"It's a complicated situation."

"Ms. Hernandez, why is it I feel every situation you deal with is complicated? Tell them to just go on in. The doors are unlocked, but they should be careful. Something happened there."

"I'm aware, and she's aware, because I believe she found that blood before you and the other owner did."

"I see."

The call ended, leaving him wondering why the woman hadn't reported the bloodstain. Maybe because she was squatting there — or was she frightened? Also, staying in such an inhospitable environment, especially with a child, made him wonder why she just didn't ask for assistance in the first place.

Maybe Whitney would have some insight. Should he call her? Spending one intimate night together did not mean they were "together".

Still, he wanted to talk to someone about it — wanted to talk to her, anyway — and maybe this was a perfect excuse.

So he called. "An after-work get-together to discuss the project? I just had an interesting call."

"I assumed we might after last night. Didn't you?"

Cal was right, he was bad at this. His reply was honest. "I hoped."

"Well, I hoped too, or last night wouldn't ever have happened. It's a date."

"So . . . no regrets?" He was probably a fool for asking but did it anyway.

"I believe it's too late for that now, isn't it?" At least there was laughter in her voice.

There were times he looked at himself in the mirror and wondered if he wasn't still stuck in high school, trying to figure out how to talk to a pretty girl. "Okay, your choice. Where and when for tonight?"

"Surprise me."

Ball straight back at him. Okay, he could play. "How about my house this time, and I'll provide the food."

His house was maybe a little cookie cutter because it was in a subdivision, but he worked quite a lot and it suited his lifestyle. Trim lawns and nice houses with straight driveways and sleek cars. He was content enough. Did he someday picture something else? He did. He liked old places with character; that's why the hotel appealed to him. A wide porch and a pleasant summer breeze . . .

"That's fine," Whitney said.

Now he had to come up with a genius plan for dinner, since he'd issued the invitation, but he could work that out. "I hope peanut butter and jelly sandwiches are okay."

"Will there be potato chips?"

"Well, of course."

"Then we're all good." Whitney laughed. "What kind of wine goes with that? This time I'll bring it."

"Oh, I think you can wing it."

The call ended, and he sat and thought about it. He decided he'd just order dinner in. He could attempt to cook — and he did now and then — but why bother? There was an Italian place down the road; it was good and they delivered.

Plan in action.

Win the girl? He hoped he was on his way.

Talk about the interesting phone call, yes. Whitney's opinion was something he valued, since her understated, intelligent approach to life appealed to him. She appealed to him, in general, if he was honest with himself about it.

Maybe she was the right woman; maybe this was a perfect storm in his normally ordered life. He had to admit he hadn't considered how it would go if he decided on pursuing a serious relationship. The quiet architect was not what he pictured, but he was starting to think it was what he wanted.

He had to call Cal. "We did have a squatter. I gave permission for her to come get the food and some personal items. She has a child."

"Oh hell. You're joking. A kid?"

"Yeah, the father called me. Accused us of kicking her out, which we did not do."

"Are you serious? *We* were the villains?"

"Could I make this up?"

"No, you don't have the imagination for it. Well, shit, what did you say?"

"I just told the truth. I told him I had no idea what he was talking about. Then I gave him the detective's number."

There was a pause. "Good call."

"The Poisoned Palace is quite a conversation piece."

"Is that the new name on the table?"

"Whitney prefers Cursed Castle. I'm debating still."

"Maybe we could vote at our next meeting."

He refrained from mentioning he and Whitney would be having a private meeting this very evening. "We should."

* * *

Dinner was very good, but by his admission, Ross didn't make it.

"Be grateful I took the shortcut. I try to cook," he admitted, "but it only turns out well sometimes. It's like rolling the dice."

Whitney just looked at him. "This is a score."

The food, laid out on an antique table that would suit the hotel dining room more than this modern house — he explained that he'd inherited it from a great aunt — made for a very enjoyable meal. Thankfully, she'd chosen the right Chianti.

"Good." It was endearing that he looked relieved. He wasn't a man who was often uncertain of himself; she'd already figured that out. After spending a night in bed with him, at least there was some equality. He knew what he was doing there, and she could define good food, because she could cook and liked to do it.

They were seeking mutual ground and finding it.

Sex and food so far.

"Dinner was very nice."

"Stay?" He looked at her with inquiring intensity.

"The night?" This was all new for her.

"I'm not very poetic, so I'll leave it up to you. In my arms, my bed, whatever you'd call it, but yes, I want to wake up next to you."

That was decently poetic as far as she was concerned. Her smile was probably tremulous. "I'm on a learning curve here."

"Is that a no or a yes?"

"A yes."

"The answer I wanted." His answering smile was spontaneous and charming.

"I'm glad you asked it."

"Whitney, if you haven't realized I'm interested, you aren't paying attention."

"The question for me is interested in what exactly."

He looked at her directly. "I could ask you the same thing."

That was a good question. She thought it over, fingering her wineglass stem, and decided to be straightforward. "I think a committed relationship and a family. Do you want children?"

"This is getting a little serious."

"Last night was serious for me."

It took a moment, as if he was considering his response. "I believe I do, with the right woman."

"I know I do, with the right man."

He took a sip from his glass. "I think we just settled that discussion, but what defines right?"

That was a fair point. "Intelligence, understanding, compassion, and someone who has a genuine desire for you?"

"Well, I've done some relatively stupid things in my life, so the 'intelligent' part of the test I might fail, but overall I think I'd pass the rest."

She had to laugh. "Ross we've all done stupid things. If I had to make a list, I'm fairly sure I would faint on the spot at the length of it."

"Hopefully last night didn't count as one of them."

"No." Her voice softened.

"I'm glad you don't count it as a mistake."

"I don't think so."

"I have zero expertise at falling in love." He was the one that said it.

"I don't either. Maybe we'll teach each other." She was verging on the hopefully romantic, but surely she was allowed that latitude.

At least it didn't seem to scare him away. "Maybe we will. So go upstairs, enjoy the differences between men and women, fall asleep, and then see what tomorrow brings?"

To a certain extent, he was right. Putting it off for so long meant her decision was weighty — was his? Well, Whitney thought, trying to be pragmatic about something that really wasn't easily analyzed, he was the one that pursued her, so maybe. "I think that sounds like a reasonable plan."

"If there is anything reasonable about relationships, you'll have to show me a chart or a graph and prove it." He stood and extended his hand. "All I know is what I really, really want right now — and that's you."

He was pretty tempting and she wasn't sure she should be doing this, but it seemed like that ship had sailed.

She put her hand in his. "Then I think we might be having a sleepover."

CHAPTER FIFTEEN

It wasn't like I didn't recognize the whiff of danger in the air, because I caught the scent and it was acrid. Our dispute had gone from disagreement to argument to downright, good old antagonism. Did I ever expect it would turn into a blood feud?

I don't know the definitive moment when it did, but it happened.

"What did you do?"

"Wheatley and I had a discussion about my barn. It might have involved my fists after he said something about you I didn't like."

I remembered I just looked at my father and wondered if that violence would be the end of it.

It wasn't.

* * *

Doreen walked over and set down a piece of paper on his desk. "You're a popular man."

Chris glanced up, but she just shook her head. "Don't ask me. I just took the message. He's persistent, I'll give him that."

He'd just gotten back from interviewing a suspect in a fraud case and was hardly in the mood for more drama. Reluctantly, he read the note.

They were aware of each other.

"This is the entire message?"

"Yep, honey."

"Same guy?"

Doreen raised a hand. "I think so. He asked me, by name, to deliver it to you."

"That was it?"

"Yep. His exact words were: 'Miss Doreen, tell Bailey this.' And then I wrote them down. This job gets a little weird now and then."

When she walked away, he sat there and stared at it, annoyed and restless. She was right. This cryptic shit was such a waste of his time . . .

Or was it?

Engaging the enemy? Maybe. The point of this escaped him. Who was aware of whom?

This game was wearing thin, since he had no idea of what this person wanted from him.

He sat there and thought about it. Disturbingly, he came up with a theory he didn't like at all.

An impossible challenge? No motive, no evidence, no reason at all it would happen? Good luck.

Except there could be a curious purpose to this.

He needed to think. He texted Anna one word. *Cabin.*

She got it, which was insightful. *Need to think?*

I do.

I can watch the moppet.

It surprised him, but he didn't want his usual solitude, so he called her. "You're invited to go with me, if you'd like."

The cabin was quaint, if nothing else. Maybe the word *worn* applied, or even *dilapidated*, but it was a very quiet setting. "Me and the moppet will pick you up."

"Sounds like a nice evening. I'll meet you at your house, if you like."

It was true; it did sound like just what he needed. So he wrapped up one last document that needed to be filed and headed home.

True to her word, Anna was already there, the moppet on a leash, a bag in hand.

She didn't ask any questions until they were in the truck and underway. "What's up?"

"I don't know. That's the problem."

"I haven't heard *that* before. How are you going to figure it out?"

"Sitting on the deck, looking at the river, and drinking beer might give me some clarity."

"I suppose that would be a relaxing venue to contemplate . . . what?"

"Bloody foyers and enigmatic messages."

"I think an idyllic setting and alcoholic beverages might be in order, if those are the subjects of the day." Anna leaned her head back against the seat and closed her eyes. "I really needed some peace and quiet, too. We're so overwhelmed right now."

"The world is a chaotic place. What's happening with the wife whose abusive husband made her lose her five kids?"

"A funny thing." Anna opened her eyes and looked at him. "He was arrested by a detective from the county sheriff's department for drug possession. He's in jail, and now she's living with her sister until we can work something else out. But she has her children back."

"I wonder how that happened."

"You were the arresting officer. I'm assuming that."

He neither confirmed or denied it. "She talked to me and told me she knew he did drugs. That's an easy arrest for anyone. One judge and a search warrant. They were there."

"Thank you."

"Thank the sheriff. Lawrence made it happen, and you should take credit as well."

"I didn't do anything."

"You told me about it."

"Well, I did do that."

"So we agree. Please tell me you'll fix dinner."

"I will. Done deal. Do you think I want to eat chili from a can?"

He had, and didn't love it. "No."

"Then trust me, my chicken fajitas will be better."

Anna had her faults, everyone did, but she was an amazing cook. "Sounds great."

What wasn't great was that the door to his cabin was cracked open when they pulled up. It was dark, but that was hardly reassuring.

"You and the moppet stay here," he said, before he drew his weapon. "I'll leave the keys in the ignition. If you hear shots fired, just drive away."

No one there, just the door open. Still, he wasn't happy.

Maybe he was careless when he closed up the cabin last, but he didn't think so. There was a routine to leaving the place, and it did not include leaving the door open.

Or an unusual knife on the floor.

He definitely didn't do that.

Cautiously, he walked through the cabin, which did not take long because it was not very big. He found it empty.

He went back out to the truck. "All clear, or sort of. I think I need an evidence bag and to take pictures. There also could be a stray raccoon or something in there, so anticipate the unexpected."

"What happened?" Anna looked understandably disturbed.

"I'm not sure, but someone has been here and apparently wanted me to know it. Let me take care of this. You and the moppet can sit on the front porch."

"All right."

So much for a cold beer and some contemplation while the river flowed quietly by. He wasn't at all pleased; maybe he needed to start locking the door. He just didn't usually. The cabin was isolated enough no one should notice it, and there was very little to steal worth the effort.

But having a weapon dumped inside his door, along with the taunting phone calls, was absolutely an invasion of his privacy, and he didn't like it.

Chris went in and snapped some pictures, sent them to Carter just in case, then used gloves and bagged up the knife, which on closer inspection had some dark substance on the blade. Why was it he thought the substance would match the dried blood at the old mansion?

Just an educated guess.

His instincts told him these things were connected. He just didn't know how.

* * *

Nice night. A starlit sky and a breeze like silk over her skin. Anna sat back and listened to the water as it rippled past, and just enjoyed the moment.

Chris, on the other hand, was predictably preoccupied. His gaze was on the river, but she doubted he really saw the view. She spoke first. "There has to be a reason."

"I agree. I need to figure it out."

"Does the knife tie the present to the history of the house?"

"It does. If that is what they're doing."

The honeysuckle was blooming; it smelled so fabulous. She crossed her ankles, enjoying her glass of wine, but thinking it over. "I don't know. I see your dilemma."

He looked relaxed, his blond hair ruffled and his expression contemplative, but he wasn't a happy man, she could tell. "I get the message, but I'm unclear on why they're trying to get my attention."

She wasn't clear on that either. "I still believe someone is taking you on."

"I don't have a crime. I can't in good conscience spend the department's money on analyzing blood samples for . . . what?"

He had a valid point.

"No, except someone did break into your cabin."

"No, they walked in. I've never locked it, which, in retrospect, is maybe too casual an approach. That decision resulted in a bad confrontation once before."

"True enough. Shall I put locks on your Christmas list?" Anna just looked at him. There were fireflies in the trees and a whippoorwill calling. Definitely a lovely evening.

"It's June. Let me think about it. I have a half of a year."

"It seems like a good idea, given some recent events."

"Anyone who wants to get into the cabin could, with or without locks. I have no neighbors."

"Which is why you like it so much."

"Yeah, that's true enough."

"I'm flattered you invited me."

"Anna, you fixed dinner. Of course I invited you. I believe you know my cooking skills are seriously in need of improvement. The food was great, by the way."

"No, your skills on *thinking* about cooking are in need of improvement. You don't care enough about it to plan ahead. I hope it wasn't the only reason you invited me."

"Not at all; hot sex is always appreciated." He gave her a boyish grin to balance out the statement. Then he added, more seriously, "I enjoy your company. I think you've already figured that out."

She enjoyed his too. That was an issue they might have to address eventually, but until his professional future was settled, she wasn't going to think about it.

"So what are you going to do?" Anna was truly curious.

"I'm weighing the options. Someone is calling me, and that someone knows me well enough that they're aware of this place. So they deposited an unwanted gift, and they might be former law enforcement — or even current, for all I know. You're the one who said they want to 'take me on'. After tonight, the challenge might be addressed. I absolutely need this place for some peace of mind. I don't need to find evidence of a crime here."

"You're personally affronted."

"Damn straight. I can dig if I have to."

"Dig how?"

"I know a few people who might be able to help me out. I'm a local boy, remember?"

She remembered he never directly answered a question, so she left it alone, with a feeling of both exasperation and amusement. "I do."

"I think I might have an angle on this." He changed the subject. "What about Kyle, Loretta, and Chloe?"

"Your house is still my best option."

He didn't object, but she felt a little guilty, because if it wasn't for their relationship, he wouldn't have two young parents and their toddler on his hands. Anna said, "I know we're imposing, but I'm having a very hard time finding the right place for them, since there's a clear threat. Sheriff Lawrence said he would send a deputy by until I could work this out, since we would be gone."

He looked surprised. "You talked to Lawrence?"

"Of course I did. If I feel like anyone is in danger, especially a child, I'm obliged to call the local authorities and tell them. I gave them your address, because it's where they're living right now."

He processed that as he did everything, without much change in expression, but with definite inner contemplation. "And I'm not there."

"According to Lawrence, your name will protect them."

"What?" He seemed truly startled.

"The locals will know they're under the umbrella of the sheriff's department."

"Because this is drug-related, and Lawrence is a man on a mission." He sounded resigned more than anything. "The moppet needs company anyway, and I'm not home very much, so they can stay until we figure it out."

"It's nice of you."

"Taking in young men in trouble with the law is apparently my new hobby."

He was referring to a case last fall, when he helped another one of her charges. "Like I said, it's nice of you. And now you've expanded your horizons to toddlers with stuffed toys."

"Chloe is pretty cute, and she seems happy. So they take good care of her, despite their age."

She agreed. "That's why I'm happy they still have her."

"I figured. Any sign of abuse or neglect and you'd be on it like a duck on a June bug."

He could make her laugh, that was part of the attraction. "Country boy, you do have a unique way of expressing yourself now and then."

"Doesn't everyone say that?"

"I don't think so."

"Huh." His mouth twitched just a little. "Well, my grandmother used to say it all the time."

"Is she still alive?" She'd met his mother, but that was about it; it hadn't even been a planned encounter.

"Yes."

That was it. No other information offered.

Anna gave up and went back to the reason they were there in first place. "It looks like a full moon. Quite romantic, and we have some privacy. Go to bed?"

He got to his feet and offered his hand. "Sounds like a plan to me."

CHAPTER SIXTEEN

Desire is an intoxicant that impairs your judgment. I know this to be true, from first-hand experience.

A ruthless competition will end badly for someone. There has to be a loser.

Sometimes it even ends badly for the winner.

Rose wrote me a love letter, and that was a mistake. Otherwise maybe I would have just been able to ignore it all.

I couldn't.

* * *

He made par on the first three holes, so Cal was having a good golf day, but playing with his dad was always a challenge.

The plans had been approved and permits for the hotel project were in the works. That was satisfying; everything was moving forward.

But it hadn't gone smoothly.

There was the unexplained bloodstain, the unwanted squatters who had occupied the house, the book Ross had received anonymously about an old vendetta centered around the place, and the possible fallout of what appeared to be a relationship between his sister and his business partner and very good friend.

"Nice shot." He watched as his father's ball arced to a landing right on the green. At one time, his father had considered going pro. He'd opted for becoming a pharmacist instead, though he did play for his college. He was good at the game but was a conservative man by nature. A more structured career suited him better than taking the gamble. Still, he was really a scratch golfer.

As casually as possible, as Cal lined up to make his long shot, he asked, "Has Whitney mentioned she's seeing Ross?"

"Is she?" His dad looked unsurprised. "Ross is a nice young man. Fine with me."

The suspicion was that they were more than "seeing each other", which was an old-fashioned phrase for dating anyway. Cal suspected, knowing Ross as well as he did, that they were already sleeping together. Ross had the ability to move fast to get what he wanted. "I've had the brotherly discussion with him."

His father laughed. "Okay, I can skip the fatherly one, then. Is it that serious?"

He swung, and of course, the ball sailed to the left of the fairway. Cal shook his head, but at the game, not the question. "I don't know. That's the problem."

"She's level-headed."

"I trust *her*."

"Not him?"

He needed to get out of the weeds in more than one way. "She's told me to mind my own business, so I will."

"Well, then keep your word. You're a lot like your mother. You want to take on the problems of the world, but that's not a realistic goal. Right now, go find your ball and get it on the green."

Easier said than done.

Both things.

"I'm not allowed to worry about my sister?"

"Of course you are, but don't interfere. I left you alone a time or two when I thought you might be making a mistake, though I wanted to impart my wisdom. You worked it out. Leave it be."

* * *

Ross was well aware he had his faults, but he hoped discourtesy wasn't one of them. When Whitney's alarm on her phone went off, he'd murmured, "You can have the shower first."

He knew she wasn't at all used to waking up in someone else's bed, and her eyes snapped open in a moment of confusion at the sound of his voice. "Oh."

"Yeah, good morning." He smoothed back her hair. "I know it is for me."

It took a moment, but she smiled and moved against him. "For me, too."

It was interesting to him that while she might be learning about physical intimacy, he was exploring unknown territory as well, with emotional attachment. "I like waking up with you in my bed."

Not particularly romantic, he thought wryly after the words were out of his mouth. Surely he could do better than that. "I meant to say—"

She stopped him with her fingertips on his lips. "I don't think either one of us knows exactly what we're doing right now, so until we have to talk about it, let's just see what happens."

That seemed like a fair deal to him and well put.

"I'll go make coffee." He slid out of bed, searched the clothes on the floor, found his jeans, and pulled them on. Then he went to fulfill his promise.

She came down fifteen minutes later in yesterday's clothes, hair damp, no cosmetics, but she didn't need them, in his opinion. "I've got to go home and get ready. There's an early meeting."

"I certainly understand that."

"Thank you for dinner."

"Last night was my pleasure, I promise you that."

She blushed, not in a girlish way but just a slight hint of pink across her cheeks. "You're certainly better at 'the morning after' than I am."

"Whitney, I don't think I'm quite as used to this as you seem to think I am."

"Well, more than me anyway."

That he had to admit, but there was still an argument to be made. "Not with someone like you."

He was grateful she didn't ask how she was different, because he wasn't sure of the answer quite yet. She merely said, "I do think I have time for a cup of coffee."

He rose with alacrity. "I'll get it."

Narrow miss there. Until he figured out how he wanted to handle this, he wasn't comfortable enough to make any kind of declaration right now. He got out a cup, poured, and set it in front of her.

"Thank you. Now tell me how you're getting along with the book."

She'd noticed the copy of *Malice Aforethought* sitting right there on his kitchen table. "Well, it's certainly interesting reading. It's about a feud between the two families."

"Maybe when you're done, let me read it?"

"I will."

She sipped her coffee — *daintily* would be how he'd describe it — and looked thoughtful. "I actually think it will make the hotel more popular. People love intrigue. They thrive on it. Look at Loch Ness. Everyone wants to see the monster. As far as I know, no one has, but people go out of their way to look. You'll have the Devil's Destination, and they'll crowd in to stay there."

He lifted his brows. "Look, if you keep changing the names, I'll lose track."

"I'm still trying for just the right one."

"When you find it, let me know." He was unwillingly amused, because the dark history of the house aside, recent events were not at all reassuring. Stray unpermitted tenants and a possible homicide were just plain unexpected problems. "I'm leaning toward just the Ivy Manor Inn."

"That's pretty generic. Let me keep pondering."

"Pondering? Okay, ponder away. You're the creative one."

* * *

No one should be able to look so good in the morning, disheveled and with a morning shadow across his jaw, yet Ross pulled it off. He made good coffee, too.

Maybe she hadn't made such a rash decision after all.

He was considerate as well. He didn't rush anything, and though she might not be long on experience, she was hardly ignorant. She knew he made an effort to ensure that she enjoyed their time in bed together.

And he'd succeeded.

She was starting to see her brother's point of view. It was clear she was in danger. Ross was undeniably attractive, and she was clearly susceptible. Good looks, intelligence, and persuasive charm. That was difficult to resist.

In fact, she hadn't resisted.

She had no idea if he really was interested in marriage and children in his future, and it was a good question to ask, but maybe after she understood where this was going.

"So, next step?" She had taken a seat across from him but had an eye on the time.

"The police have gathered everything they need, and we have the plans thanks to you, the permits. So we move forward with the construction."

"That sounds like a plan to me."

"This is now Cal's ship to sail. He's in charge. I just handle the financial part."

"Is that all?" she said dryly. "I don't know that you got the easier role. It seems from an outsider perspective that you complement each other quite well on a project like this."

"I agree, and I need to thank him for bringing you into it."

Smooth, but she thought he was sincere, even though she was still mindful they both were being cautious — for different reasons — about their relationship. He might be reluctant about falling in love and she was fairly sure she was already traveling that path. Different speeds.

Would they find common ground was the real question.

She opted for a neutral statement. "I'm apparently on board with it."

"I'm glad you are," he said softly.

They just looked at each other.

She glanced at her watch. "I have to go."

"I need to get moving, too. I think I miscalculated when I didn't suggest we just shower at the same time."

"And that would have been faster?"

"Probably not, but a lot more enjoyable."

He did have a wicked, sexy smile.

"Another morning, then." She got up and took her cup to the sink. Yes, she was in trouble, so it was prudent just to leave and think it all over.

* * *

The trip to the office was contemplative.

When she got to work she found Will had left a note on her desk. *Come see me.*

That was not exactly usual. Since he was a senior partner, she usually asked if she could see *him* if she needed something.

He was notorious for getting to work early, so it was no surprise he was already at his desk in his office.

"Good morning. You wanted to see me?"

"Whitney. Yes, I do." His affable smile was always a good part of her day. "I have something for you, or more specifically, for your good friend Mr Waylan."

Will pointed to a large envelope on his desk. "Here's all the information the historical society has on his house. We do expect it back, so it's on loan. There are newspaper clippings, the original deed, photographs, and so forth."

"Understood." She was aware some things could not be replaced, so he'd gone to some effort; she appreciated it. "Ross and Cal will be careful and return it all. Thank you."

"Could you ask if I can drop by now and then and see how the restoration and renovation are going? I might be able to offer some advice, if there are questions on authenticity."

That really was generous of him. "I'm sure they would agree to that in a heartbeat. They want it to be done period but be comfortable. To keep it authentic, but with the modern amenities it needs to make sure guests are happy. I'm sure your insights would be invaluable."

"I'd be glad to help. I'm very interested in this project."

She was, too. Coming up with the design and plans had been an enjoyable challenge. "I already know the answer is yes, so I don't have to ask. Both Cal and Ross will appreciate the input."

When she got back to her desk, it was nice to be able to text her brother: *Lots of cooperation from the historical society. I have the paperwork.*

When her phone beeped, she was sure it was him, so she absently ignored the display, because she had other work to do. When she did glance at it, it wasn't at all what she expected.

Call Detective Bailey and ask him about what happened to Riley.

That set her back. What?

She sat there, stymied and indecisive. Instead of Cal, she called Ross. Hesitantly, she said, "Hi. Sorry to bother you at work. I just got the most unusual message. I'm supposed to call Detective Bailey about someone named Riley. Who is Riley? Any clue?"

"No, but now I'm alarmed. You don't need to be pulled into this . . . this . . . I don't know exactly what to call it."

"Situation? It seems like I am involved, by virtue of association."

"Maybe, but I still don't like it. I'll call Detective Bailey and tell him."

"No, I'm a big girl and can handle it myself, but thanks for the offer. He might have questions. I need his number. I assume you have it."

"I'll send it right now." He paused. "I'm fine if you prefer to handle it, but I don't like this at all. Why text you?"

"I don't understand any of it, but maybe the detective will."

"The problem is, I don't think he does yet either. Let me know what he says, please."

She called and left a message. It took a while, but the detective did call her back. "Thank you for getting in touch with me. Can you tell me anything else about this text? Anything at all?"

"It wasn't really threatening, just disturbing. It told me to call you. I have the phone number."

"I have a feeling I do too, but give it to me, please. Riley? Well, at least I have a name to work with."

He sounded grim, which wasn't reassuring. She'd recited the number and he politely thanked her, but she was left with a feeling of disquiet.

Someone knew she was associated with the house project. How they got her cell number was a mystery, but they obviously managed it.

The question was, had they also managed to get away with murder?

CHAPTER SEVENTEEN

The burial spot is symbolic.
> *Of course it is. A sign of imminent death, a reminder of mortality.*
> *Mine was unremarkable.*
> *A simple spot in a remote place where no one would look.*
> *That was the point of the whole event.*

* * *

Someone was playing a game, and it wasn't a pleasant one.

Chris wasn't sure of the goal, but he was a part of it. The phone call from Ms. Nolte cemented that. She was able to give him a specific name. It was like someone was spoon-feeding him obscure clues.

He was starting to get irritated with this game.

He scoured the missing person reports and found nothing on anyone named Riley, first name or last.

Maybe this was a cold case.

But he had a new problem, because the blood in that old house had not long been there when he'd walked in.

And who was this Lattrell? He couldn't get a handle on that, either. It could be an alias, the badge a bit of fiction, but Kyle had seen the gun and said he wore it like a police officer.

What the hell was going on?

He felt like Kyle was telling him the truth, mainly because he genuinely seemed afraid for Loretta and Chloe and desperate to protect them. He'd also taken responsibility for his choices; when they'd met with Lawrence his story had held up to some sharp inquiries with raw honesty. Chris could tell the sheriff had decided to not charge him, even with an open admission of guilt, because the young man was cooperating and he was after the big fish, not the small fry. Those were his words. Angling was one of his hobbies.

Meth labs were a worse problem, but the state of Tennessee still had not legalized marijuana either. On a criminal level, it was not a high crime, but it was part of a bigger problem.

Kyle had been able to provide the destination of the product, if not any knowledge of who was going to pick it up. The details of the exchange included no identities, but at least they had a location.

Lawrence never said it, but it was there in the room: *What are you going to do about this?*

If only Chris knew.

Hopefully, he'd figure it out, but he hadn't yet.

"What's going on?" Carter came by his desk. "I know that abstracted look on your face. Did the meeting with Lawrence not go well?"

"No, it was fine. Kyle cooperated and maybe gave us some good information. But here's another question." Carter had been with the department a long time, and Chris was about to consult his hard-won fund of knowledge. "Does the name 'Riley' ring a bell with you?"

"I don't know."

"Well, I don't know either. That's why I'm asking you."

"As in George Riley?" Carter looked thoughtful. "He ran against Lawrence years ago for sheriff. Lost, obviously. He became a deputy instead, for a different county, and was decent at it as far as I know. We interacted a few times on crossover cases. He quit a few years ago, I think."

At last, maybe a break. "Older guy?"

To give him credit, Carter started to get seriously interested. "Between us in age. I would guess in his forties. What's this about?"

Chris leaned his elbows on the desk. "Someone connected with the case got a text telling them to ask me what happened to 'Riley'. This person contacted me, but the name didn't mean anything until maybe right now."

"How so?" Carter took a seat. "Enlighten me."

"The person running drugs with Kyle claims to be a law enforcement officer, or that's what Kyle said. Actually, he claimed the guy had a badge, which in a past tense, could be quite true." Chris had to pause. "I just don't understand why he'd bring himself to our attention."

"If it is him. It could be someone else."

It wasn't like it hadn't occurred to him. "Yeah, I know, but why?"

"*Who.*"

They were destined to have this ongoing argument. "Fine, I know your point of view: who? But I want to know why they would bother. Him or anyone else."

"If I had to speculate, just thinking in a linear fashion, your young friend Kyle is the premium suspect to have killed Riley, because he showed up and threatened him. Maybe he was defending his girlfriend and child, and then ran, after disposing of the body."

It did make for a likely scenario, except he didn't think that was what happened. Chris shook his head. "I don't think he's lying to us. I can tell you for sure he isn't the one making these phone calls, because it isn't his voice. Someone else still alive is involved. Surely we can find Riley. A former deputy? We can at least talk to him."

"He's more canny than that. He won't tell us a thing, if he's involved."

"Let's find him. That should be easy enough, and I want to hear his voice and figure out if he's the one that's been calling me."

"I have to admit the purpose of that escapes me."

"Engaging the enemy. That's Anna's theory."

"How are you the enemy?"

"Good question. There's not even a crime I'm aware of, but he's dumping a bloody knife at my cabin and calling people to deliver messages to me, so we aren't exactly friends."

Carter frowned. "None of this makes sense."

"No, but somebody with an interesting agenda thinks it does."

"Doreen probably has access to Riley's address, or at least his last one. Let's start there." His partner stood in a decisive motion.

Chris didn't disagree. Any connection would help. If George Riley was Lattrell, maybe they'd at least have a lead. If the man would admit it — which he also doubted, if the man was a former deputy. But it was worth following the possibility.

There was still no actual crime, besides some evidence in an unlocked cabin, which indicated trespassing. Processing DNA didn't happen in an instant, and Chris needed a good reason to ask for it.

He didn't have one yet.

Doreen was predictably helpful. "I'll call that county and get the address. I know Jill pretty well. She'll give it to me."

Of course she did. She knew everyone in the state, as far as Chris could tell. "It would be appreciated."

Minutes later, she deposited it on his desk with a flourish. "Here you go, darlin'."

"Thanks." He wasn't positive how much he wanted to go after this former law enforcement officer in case someone was just implicating him, but it was all he had.

Who knew if this would pay off in any way? But he'd take even a slim lead.

* * *

"There's a body in the basement."

Ross glanced up from his desk. "What?"

Cal came into the office and didn't sit down or even say hello. "Apparently one of the construction crew found it, to his horror, behind an antique organ he was trying to move out. The foreman of the crew called me — after he called the police, of course — to inform me of this delightful new development in the Hotel of Horrors."

"You have to be kidding me. Shit." Ross was not happy at all with this unwelcome news to say the least.

"I'm not kidding at all. You didn't talk to the man. He's understandably horrified and wants us there right away to handle it."

Ross pushed a button to shut down his computer. "Let's go."

"I agree."

They it to the SUV in record time, and Cal spun out of the parking lot.

Ross buckled up, and tried to take this information in.

"Behind . . . what? An organ? We have an organ and a corpse in the basement? What is *that* about?"

"Right. Good question. So the House from Hell is continuing the legacy?" Cal just shook his head, concentrating on breaking the speed limit.

"It seems like it."

"I'm pretty sure that young workman is going to decline to return to this construction project."

"Who could blame him? Do we have details?"

"'Body' is about all I have. They're a construction crew, not forensic experts."

"Let's see what we're dealing with."

"Dead person in a dark abandoned basement? I think I've seen that movie. I don't know if I'm up for this, but we certainly need to talk to the crew."

Ross said reflectively, "A decomposing human body has a definite odor, as I understand it, though I'm happy to have never experienced it first-hand. How could anyone have missed it?"

Cal didn't look thrilled with that observation. "I didn't go down there, so I don't know. It seemed to me the detective that came for the bloodstain thought the blood trail was out of the house, not into it. I agree it looked like that to me, too."

"No, it has to be someone else."

"I hope not."

That would be great, Ross thought grimly. Two murders? If there was even a first. They had no idea. Just the same, it didn't sound very promising.

The drive emphasized the beauty of the countryside setting but it did nothing to help the situation. Green trees and blue skies, but no inner contentment. Wildflowers and wispy horsetail clouds, yet none of that helped the feeling of apprehension.

The house looked as usual, except for the men sitting outside doing nothing and the police car. Apparently no one wanted to be inside with a dead body — fine, Ross didn't blame them.

They parked, and he looked at Cal. "We'll go to the cellar, see what we're dealing with."

"I'll talk to the foreman while you handle that. God, I don't want to do this."

Ross had to agree. "I'd rather be sitting down to an only somewhat cold beer at the Cactus, like when we were in college, but here we are. Let's go see what we've got."

Silence. No one seemed to know what to say as they walked up. Quite frankly, neither did he or Cal. Finally, he spoke to the assembled group. "Behind an organ? Didn't know we had one. I hope you didn't touch anything."

"A small instrument way back in the left corner. I thought it was a spinet piano until I went to move it." The young man who spoke was about twenty or so, with rumpled brown hair and a shaky smile. "I move pianos as a side job. I have to admit, I about passed out when I saw what was behind it. And as far as touching it, no. You couldn't pay me enough for that."

That might help the police, anyway. "We'll handle this." Cal sounded calm and assured, but Ross knew he was not at all interested in going downstairs, any more than he was.

Dark stairs and no lights; it didn't sound like fun. Jeff, the foreman, handed over a powerful flashlight. "I've handled a lot of jobs, but nothing like this. Plumbing, electricity, drywall . . . I can do it. Dead bodies, not so much. The officers are there." He pointed.

It was not beautiful going down the questionable steps, like descending into a tomb. Most of the big furniture had been moved, so it was just dim and cluttered.

They were stopped by a deputy until they identified themselves as the owners of the property.

And yes, there was a dead body, but it was hardly new. The face sunken, hands curled like claws, it was gruesome, and clearly not a fresh corpse. Decomposition had set in some time ago. One of the officers asked, "Identification? Any idea who he is?"

Cal looked like he was about to lose it, so Ross said firmly, "No."

"When the detectives arrive, we'll remove the body."

It was a dismissal, and he was happy enough to get it. When they went back upstairs, they just looked at each other.

"Jesus," Cal said, running his hand over his face.

"Whoever's blood was in the foyer, it was not from that person." Ross didn't need a medical degree to come to that conclusion. He welcomed the late afternoon sun streaming in through the tall — though still dirty — windows. The warmth and light did help to balance out his disturbed state of mind.

Ross had to admit that when they'd looked at the house, he'd just glanced over the basement, saw it was still full of furniture and didn't go over every nook and cranny. That body had been there for a while.

He took out his phone and called Detective Bailey instead of Doreen, since he suspected Bailey would be the one who had to respond.

"Look, this is Ross Waylan and I'm at the house. I assume they've called you."

"I'm just pulling in. Stay there, in case I have some questions."

Then he called Whitney. "I might be occupied this evening."

"Oh, is she prettier than me or something?"

"No one is prettier than you, and no, you aren't even remotely on target as to why."

"I was just teasing you, but nice compliment. What's wrong?"

"Depending on how long this takes, maybe I'll tell you over a glass of wine."

CHAPTER EIGHTEEN

The parallel between good and evil escapes me.

Since no one is all good and no one is all bad, usually, then we walk the middle line. I felt I was mostly good with solid principles, but I'm not sure the world viewed me that way.

My death set off a series of events I wasn't really responsible for, but yet I was held accountable, to the extent that if I hadn't acted in a certain way, none of it might have happened.

No one is sorrier than me.

Except maybe Rose.

* * *

Chris got out of his vehicle and looked at the old house, feeling resigned that this was not going to be a pleasant experience.

Body in the basement? Not an emergency. Evidently the body wasn't new, which meant the coroner wasn't necessary right away. Looking at dead bodies was hardly his favorite pastime.

It'd been a long day, but he had signed on for this occupation.

Both of the owners were waiting for him, sitting on the rickety steps, drinking beer. They stood as he walked up. Cal Nolte informed him, "The beer was necessary."

"Sometimes it is." He confirmed the sentiment. "Okay, take me to this happy find."

Steep cellar steps, dark and not necessarily any safer than the porch — he'd been down them once before, but just for a quick look. There had been no fresh blood, so at the time he'd been checking to see if anyone was down there, even though that had been near to impossible with all the jumbled furniture and boxes and no lights. Now that it had been partially cleared out, he could see the organ. Two deputies greeted his arrival with relief.

"Good to see you, Detective." The older one nodded and shook his head. They'd known each other for quite a while now. "I'm damned glad you're here."

"Tom, what do we have?"

"Nothing good. Take a look. We haven't touched a thing."

In the dim flashlight beam, it looked gruesome. And it certainly wasn't a recent death. No question that body had been there a while.

They needed the coroner, because the medical examiner would have to get involved. Their offices were connected, plus someone had to take the body away.

He reluctantly made the call to Carter. "Talk to Loren and tell him I have a body. Been around for a while, so he can take his time, but I think it needs to go to the ME. Someone hid it in the cellar of an empty house. Let's find out what happened from a cause of death."

"I think we're supposed to do that."

"Yeah, I do too. Part of the job description. Dr Loren will be thrilled with the Gothic setting. It's a lot like I imagine the basement of Dracula's castle."

"*You* don't sound thrilled."

"I'm not. Be glad you were working that other case."

Chris went upstairs and found the owners back on the front steps. He sat down as well. "Now we wait for the coroner. All three of us realize he's dead, whoever he is, but our opinion doesn't matter. The coroner will say yep, we're correct, and he'll take the body away. The medical examiner will give a cause of death as well as an opinion on the manner of death."

Ross Waylan looked at him. "The difference being?"

"Manner of death being whether it was homicide, accidental, or natural causes."

"I see. Not a cop, so I didn't know the distinction."

"What do you know about the former owners?"

The sun was starting to be more of a glimmer than an active presence as dusk descended. "The heirs sold it to a couple that gave it back to the bank for personal reasons," Cal Nolte said. "So we know nothing."

"I know some about the history of the house," Waylan offered, "thanks to a book about this place. It does not have the happiest legacy ever. The book was sent anonymously, meaning someone was paying attention to the fact that this house was sold, and to who bought it."

That was interesting.

"After the medical examiner makes a determination, I might request that information from you. It depends on the resulting investigation." Chris wasn't sure it would be helpful, but as always any information was welcome.

Murder was one thing, but if the man in the basement died from natural causes and someone just didn't want to pay to bury him, so they left the body in an abandoned house . . . well, then the case fell to the bottom of the list.

Except he was sure someone hid that body for a purpose that didn't promise a pleasant result for the autopsy. He wouldn't go willingly into that dark space. He'd have left it in the woods, or something similar, unless there was a crime involved. Neither he nor Carter needed another case, but if he was a betting man, he would wager they were going to be handed one.

"You two don't have to wait for Dr Loren to arrive. This won't take long. We'll have Forensics come take a look tomorrow, but I don't think this was the crime scene, if there was one at all. I'll let you know what's going on."

No argument. He didn't blame them. Waylan went over to his vehicle and came back with a beer. "We both needed a cold one. If you want this, go ahead; if not, just leave it."

"Oh, I'll take it. I have no idea how long I'll be here. Nice of you."

They departed quietly, and he didn't blame either one of them. He'd leave if he could. There were more enjoyable pastimes to be had than waiting for the coroner. Anna would be fixing dinner right about now.

But at least he had a beer, so he cracked it, thinking hard. Loretta would not be able to help, and he wasn't anxious to tell her she'd been sleeping — with her young child — in a house with a decomposing body. That corpse had been there a while, so he was reluctant to ask her if she had any idea it was in the basement. If she did, she'd have told him already, he figured.

Loren rolled up in the usual van faster than expected and got out with a deputy and a resigned look on his face. "My wife is making her infamous chicken casserole for dinner, so thank you for the call, Detective. She thinks it's delicious. I'm not a fan, but have yet to share that opinion in all the years we've been married. Let's go see what we have."

"You'll lose your appetite, trust me, so you won't have to lie about not being hungry. Follow me."

Back to the dank basement with the body in it. He pointed at the organ. "Behind that. The body hasn't been disturbed that I know of. We haven't touched it, but with just a flashlight I couldn't see an obvious cause of death. The construction crew moved the organ, but then ran for the hills when they saw what was behind it."

Loren was an extremely pragmatic man. "I'll take a look. That's why I'm here."

It certainly did not take long before the stretcher and body bag were put to use and the remains removed, Chris helping to carry them out, not anxious to stay in the dismal space any longer than necessary. It was a relief to step outside and navigate the treacherous porch, even with their grisly burden.

The body was loaded into the van, and Loren summed it up succinctly. "I couldn't see an obvious cause either, but the subject appears young for natural causes. The location of the body, too, is suspicious. Let's see what the autopsy tells us. The ME can take it from here, and the rest is up to you."

Lucky him. "Sounds like a bit of a challenge," Chris said dryly. "Natural causes or not, who put him there on purpose? There has to be a reason, and I doubt it's a happy one."

"I can tell you one thing that might help. I believe I know who he is."

"Are you serious?"

Loren smiled thinly. "Am I ever not serious? I think even as little as he looked this afternoon like he did in life, that is George Riley. I knew the man. Right height, build, and facial definition, even distorted by the inevitable changes brought on by death."

Riley? Well, if it was true, that was at least a break. He needed one, and it must have shown. "You're sure? Why would a man who once wanted to be sheriff be dead in the basement of an abandoned house?"

"No, not sure, just an impression. I firmly believe there are times you're relieved to not be me, but this is a case of vice versa. I hope you figure it out, Detective, and otherwise, have a good evening."

* * *

Since she wasn't sure if she had evening plans or not, Whitney just worked on some drawings at the desk in her home office and contemplated how, in such a short amount of time, she'd gotten used to having someone to share a meal and conversation with.

Not to mention a bed.

It was nice to hear his breathing at night. Though she had never minded living alone, having a lover was a revelation in ways that went beyond an intimate physical relationship. Ross added an interesting dynamic to her life she hadn't even known was missing. She'd always been reserved, and he had the ability to draw her out and make her laugh. She was comfortable around him.

So when he texted, she saw the number and read it immediately.

In your driveway.

She went to the front door. Sure enough, Ross was there, and he'd brought food *and* wine. He got out of the vehicle with bags in hand, his expression not exactly happy. "I've not had the most pleasant day. Food and alcohol seem in order. I hope you agree."

"From the look on your face, you deserve both." She stood back to let him in.

"Did Cal call you?"

"No, not yet."

"So he's counting on me to tell you, then. Just wait until you hear the story, but let's open the wine first."

He took care of that while she got out plates, unwrapped the food, and set the table.

He came to sit and handed her a glass of something red. "For dinner, I just asked for something good. I don't even know what we're having."

"It looks like panini of some kind."

"I can fly with that."

She suspected he could fly with anything, if he could forget about current circumstances.

The sandwiches were delicious and the wine was smooth, so Whitney waited and sipped her drink until he was ready to tell her.

Worth waiting for the dramatic impact.

"There was a body in the house, behind an old organ in the basement."

Not what she expected. Incredulously, she said, "What?"

"I know. I wish I knew how to describe it, but then again I wouldn't. It was hardly pretty; you don't need the details."

"So, the blood in the in foyer—"

"Nope," he interrupted, shaking his head. "I'm hardly an expert, but this body had been there a while."

It took her a moment, but finally Whitney said, "I can't believe no one noticed before now. And, secondly, you have an organ in the basement? Did Edgar Allen Poe write this story?"

He smiled wryly. "I agree on both counts. The organ is small, maybe for a chapel or something, but still the size of an upright piano. I didn't study it too closely, because I was looking at the dead person on the floor behind it. The house sat empty for a long time, so that's probably why no one noticed. When we looked at it, we didn't tour the basement either. It's dark and cluttered with discarded furniture, so we skipped it."

She could see that. "I suppose I might have skipped it too, but you had the home inspected, right?"

"Yes we did. I think we failed to ask him to look behind the old organ to see if there might be a body there."

Whitney ignored the sarcasm. "So the Macabre Manor theme continues. What did the police say?"

He took a very long drink from his glass. "Detective Bailey told Cal and me we could leave, because he was waiting for the coroner. So we both left. What could we do? We'd be just standing there with our hands in our pockets, unable to help."

She'd have left as well, rather than just stay around. She knew Cal would have been out of there in a heartbeat. The sight of that pool of blood had about sent him over the edge. He was a man of action. If it was out of his skill set, he hated that he couldn't fix it immediately.

The man sitting across from her was more contemplative than her brother. "I can't imagine who he would be. No one has lived there in years."

"The dead person? Maybe have Cal ask Beth. She's so into crime, she follows those stories."

He looked surprised. "Does she? I thought she was a librarian."

"She's also the daughter of a police officer." Whitney remembered well the various books scattered across the apartment they'd shared in college, among them a treasured copy of *In Cold Blood* that was actually signed by Capote.

There was a part of her that wondered if the attraction to Cal had something to do with him now owning a house with such a dark history. "She isn't morbid, she just finds it . . . fascinating. That's a good way to describe it."

"I'll mention it to Cal, but he was not a fan of the whole thing."

"Who would be?"

"I know I'm not."

"So talk to her. She's extremely smart, that much I can promise you. Research is her deal."

He regarded her over the table. "Do you mind if I give her the book first?"

The one someone sent to him? "No, do it. She might be able to connect the dots, if they're there to connect."

"That's not a bad idea."

It wasn't. Beth was interested in, and knowledgeable about, anything that was remotely suspicious in the surrounding areas. It was a hobby, not her living, but there was a chance she might know something.

"I'm in love with you."

Whitney had no idea what to say, it was so unexpected. It came out of the blue — probably did for Ross as well as her.

Luckily, Ross did know what to say. "No, don't respond in any way. I'm not ready for it either. Can we both just go to bed and talk about it later?"

CHAPTER NINETEEN

In the great scheme of all things, death is simply an aggravation. One plane to the other is an inconvenient restructuring of your existence, but not overwhelming.

It's more that he lost the battle.

He was vanquished and I managed to get even from the grave. There was some satisfaction in that.

* * *

The old, turn-of-the-century library building was quiet, dust motes floating through the air, shelves to the ceiling — he could see the appeal of it. Ross was never opposed to solitude. Beth Garret came into the room, looking reserved in a sweater over a conservative dress; it was cool in there first thing in the morning.

"Thanks for taking the time."

"Of course I would. I got your email."

Brisk and professional, but curious. All the things he wanted. He showed her the book. "Someone is sending me a message, clearly about the history of the house, but I need another perspective. According to Whitney, this is your sort of thing."

She examined the book. "Indeed it is. Where did you get this?"

"It was a gift from an unknown source."

"Richard Gothard is pretty hard to track down. It had to be a pen name. I've been looking without much luck so far. This is a pretty old volume." She turned it over. "I don't even recognize the publisher, and they didn't give a date of publication."

"I think my question for you is: how would someone get ahold of it?"

"I would think they inherited it or got it from an older relative. This was not widely published, obviously, but I do know who to ask."

"It's nice to know you and Whitney. You both have connections. A forensic librarian? I thought Cal and I just bought an old house to restore and put to good use again. It's becoming a lot more complicated than that."

"Isn't the history of it fascinating, though?"

It was getting even more so, though he wished it wasn't quite so dark. "Interesting, yes, if you're into murder and mayhem. We didn't know about that when we bought it." The agreement was made with that caveat. He doubted Cal had mentioned their recent grim find, but the history of the house was indeed fraught with conflict and strife. "I'd really like to know who took the time and trouble to send me this book. If you could narrow the field a little, I believe I know a detective who would be very grateful for the information."

"A detective?" Beth looked quite startled.

"Ask Cal about it. In the meantime, if having the book will help, you can read it. That why I stopped by, so you could actually look at it."

She glanced up at him, her expression serious. "Put it in a glass case in the lobby of the hotel. For all we know, this is the only copy that still exists."

And someone sent it to him.

Why?

He walked out to his car, thinking it over.

Then there was the matter of the body hidden in the basement.

Not to mention the bloody foyer.

What the hell?

And there was him, not just enjoying a sexual relationship, but having a love affair. He'd even said it out loud.

Life had gotten out of hand. He was much more used to being on an even keel, where he controlled where he was headed.

That was definitely slipping.

He drove back to the office and found, to his surprise, someone was waiting for him, drinking a cup of coffee in his office.

Detective Carter looked deceptively relaxed. "Your receptionist offered, and I'm glad I said yes. The coffee here is a lot better than in the sheriff's office." He took an envelope out of his pocket and extracted some photographs. "I have a few questions. Can you identify any of these men?"

"I want to help in any way I can." Ross sorted through the photos. Out of six, he did recognize one. "This looks like the realtor who sold us the house."

"Peter Johnson?"

"Yes."

"That was months ago."

Ross registered the implication. "Yes, we signed months ago and we did get the keys, and no, I haven't seen him since because our business was finished at the closing. It took time to get things into place to do the improvements. So it sat empty."

"Have you seen him since?"

Oh hell. Ross had to absorb that for a moment. "He was the dead man we found?" It hadn't looked like him, but then again, death surely did you no favors.

Carter simply said, "No, we don't think so. We just want to know if you recognize any of his business associates."

Ross took a second look and then shook his head. "No, I'm afraid not. I thought he was an independent agent."

"When it came to real estate, I think he was."

The light started to dawn. "So maybe not so in other areas?"

"We doubt it."

"And he was using the house?"

"What do you think? He didn't sell it for a long time, because he didn't actually list it as active."

Good point.

"I did have to call about it," Ross said, "because there was no indication it had sold, but I couldn't find it online as the sale of a house, just as land. That's how Cal found it. He was looking for property and went there and saw the house. There was no sign near the road, so I called the agency and talked to someone who probably was a secretary. She told me it was bank-owned and gave me their number."

"So he *had* to show it then." It seemed like Carter was thinking out loud now.

Ross thought about it. "That makes sense, I suppose, to use a deserted house if you have first-hand knowledge it's secluded and empty. Any idea what he was using it for?"

"We do." Carter was apparently just as unwilling to disclose details as his partner. "Since there seems to be recent activity, keep us informed if anyone sees or has evidence of anything suspicious. You just connected one of the points that had us puzzled, which is why he finally decided to actually do his job and put it on the market."

Recent activity? What did that mean? The pool of blood?

"Please tell me no more bodies will pop up."

Detective Carter got to his feet. "How can I promise that? The bad guys are in charge right now, but Detective Bailey and I would like to shift the dynamic, if possible. Thanks for the coffee, and we'd appreciate a call if anything comes to your attention."

* * *

Chris had not one but two cases that really needed work, so he wasn't opposed to letting Carter handle questioning Ross

Waylan. It wasn't as if he was in charge, particularly, as lead. When it came down to it, Carter had the upper hand most of the time and justly so. He'd been doing this longer.

"That didn't gain us much." His partner came and sat in the chair on the other side of the desk. "Waylan knew our missing person right away but didn't recognize anyone else. He did provide an explanation for why the house was finally listed and sold, and that was because he called the bank about it directly."

So the bank realized it wasn't listed. Interesting, but not really helpful to the investigation.

"It was a long shot, and we both knew it. That's an investment property, nothing else, to both him and Nolte. Peter Johnson was never reported missing but quit showing up at his office. His mother lives in California and only talked to him infrequently. That he was killed seems pretty clear, but we're still left with whose blood that was just inside the door."

"No. Lawrence is rabid over this, because he thinks drugs are involved."

"Well, we know they could be. There was some reason Johnson didn't provide an active listing for the house and let it sit empty so long."

"So are we thinking someone killed him because he finally sold it?"

Carter rubbed his jaw, obviously thinking it over. "Well, he knew whatever was going on was illegal, and he was getting a cut, or he wouldn't have been stalling the bank and pretending he was doing his best to sell the property. It was brilliant, in that it isn't the easiest property to market — in disrepair and out of the line of sight from the road — so the bank took his word for it. I guess our real question is, why did he make that fatal decision?"

It wasn't like Chris hadn't asked himself that same question. "If you don't realize you're swimming with sharks, you might get eaten," he said grimly. "I bet the bait was tempting, and he didn't quite get who he was dealing with."

"Small fish devouring other small fish, or something bigger?"

"Right. We can't take on organized crime. We aren't staffed for it, and they know it."

"Well, federal law enforcement can. We just have to give them something, but all we have is one body and a bloody handprint."

Carter agreed. "The medical examiner's report will help."

"When it gets to us. He's busy, but what's new? Would you want to be one?"

"An ME? No. But would you want to be us?"

"More than him, absolutely." Chris disliked the morgue intensely. "We hunt. He tells us what kind of animal we're hunting for. So let's go over that report and see if it gives us anything."

"Well, someone hid that body."

"Cause of death and manner of death will be somewhat helpful, but we still have no idea what was going on."

They really didn't. *Clueless* took on a whole meaning. He'd had cases with too many suspects, but in this one, it was barren soil without a weed in it. No suspect at all.

Maybe Lawrence was wrong on this one. Not drug-related, but tied to something else? It was possible.

"Contraband of some sort?"

"It could be. Lots of space and cover to move it."

"We're speculating."

"Oh yes, we are. No evidence."

"Didn't your houseguest mention hearing all kinds of noises?" Carter asked Bailey.

"Big house. Not surprising. She has a young child. She didn't go look to see what was happening. I don't blame her either. Loretta hid from me, and I made it verbally clear I was a police officer."

"Not everyone likes to hear that, especially when they're breaking the law."

A point he couldn't argue. "She doesn't know anything. I'm sure enough of it. She'd tell me; she's living in my house. After I left the note, she did reach out."

"Safe haven doesn't mean total honesty."

Maybe not, but his instincts said she *was* being honest. "I've asked her."

"So what we need is the body of someone killed recently."

"That, unfortunately, would help us, if we can identify them."

"If we can *find* them. Lots of possibilities out there."

It turned out there were.

Timing was everything. Doreen walked over and set down a piece of paper on Chris's desk. "You have a floater in a quarry nearby. You two get the privilege of checking it out. There's supposedly a knife wound in his chest. What the heck? I'm moving to California and marrying a movie star. It is too crazy around here. I need a more sedate life."

"And here we were just hoping for a victim." Chris wished he was joking, but both he and Carter were already on their feet. "Do you have anyone in mind for your future husband?"

"I'm thinking it over." She headed back to her desk.

They walked out together and Carter got out the keys. "I'll drive, you navigate."

"That's fine with me."

There was no address, just a general description of the property, but it was county-owned, so there were several deputies there already and a state police car as well. They pulled up and were greeted with grim faces and brief nods.

The body wasn't a pleasant sight. The victim was naked; if this had been a skinny-dipping adventure, it had ended badly.

That knife in his cabin . . .

Decomposition looked right for the timing, but he wasn't a forensic expert. Chris had an eye for it from experience, but no expertise.

The knife had been obviously a stiletto or, more aptly described, a dagger. Long blade, and not meant for anything else besides harm to another human being. The average person didn't own one, so maybe they were facing organized crime.

That was an unpleasant hypothesis.

"Johnson?"

"That'd be my guess. Well, we have the blood sample from the floor, so we'll have an answer about whether he was killed in the house when the DNA comes back." Next to him, his expression shuttered, Carter was as straightforward as ever. "They took his identification, a signature for a professional hit."

"And our missing realtor seems to have stopped showing up at the office; his secretary finally got worried enough to call. This is getting complicated as hell, but truthfully, we don't have very many homicides.."

"Not very many homicides?" Chris disagreed. "We've been on a pretty solid run lately."

Carter gave him a look, but then relented. "Let me restate. I've been doing this job for a long time, and usually I'm not working multiple homicide cases."

Chris looked at the unfortunate scenery. "I think you are now."

CHAPTER TWENTY

They hanged him, and it was justified. Tennessee justice is not necessarily governed by laws put down by politicians and law enforcement because sometimes it's necessary to just make things right the old-fashioned way.

Eye for an eye.

We have our own sense of right and wrong here in these hills and hollows. So they strung him up.

I approved from my cold grave.

After all, he'd killed me.

* * *

Was there anything more awkward than dropping off a gift for your ex-husband's new child, the one he just had with your best friend?

Anna was fairly sure the answer was no as she pulled into the driveway, but Trey was a busy man, so maybe he wouldn't be there.

Of course, he answered the door.

Just her luck.

"Hi." That wasn't brilliant, so she tried again. "Congratulations. Steph called me with the news. I just brought a gift for the baby."

"She's feeding him right now, but I'm sure she wouldn't mind your company."

"No. I won't bother her. I'll give it to you and tell her I'll come by later."

He looked fantastic like he always did, with his dark rumpled hair and those vivid eyes — but, to her satisfaction, he also looked a little tired. "When I'm not here, is that it?"

She was finding peace with it all, but he was right. "Pretty much. Do you blame me?"

"Anna . . ."

She set down the bag and walked away. There were some things that required distance, and this was one of them.

The middle ground still didn't exist.

At least she'd been moderately polite.

She got in her car and cried as she pulled away, but it wasn't much. A trickle down her cheek for what they'd lost, but so it went. Some things weren't meant to be.

Chris was right to be wary that she was still hung up on her ex, but she was pretty into him, too, and he was leaving her.

There didn't seem to be any tropical sunsets on her horizon.

* * *

Chloe greeted him with enthusiasm, carrying her beloved stuffed toy. Chris was getting more comfortable with his apparent honorary uncle status, and so he picked her up when she lifted her arms. "Hi."

She hugged him, and the moppet also jumped up on him, and the effusive welcome helped dissipate some of the grim reality of his day. The smell of something pretty fantastic coming from the kitchen didn't hurt either.

He carried Chloe through and found Anna at the stove, whisking away at some sauce, and from the set of her shoulders, she was using cooking as therapy. Usually a good outcome for him, but it meant maybe she'd had a hard day. He set Chloe on her feet and she scampered off, presumably to find her mother, the dog in tow. If nothing else, his houseguests provided company for the dog, because sometimes he worked long days.

By way of greeting, he said, "I don't know what you're fixing, but it smells great."

Anna glanced over her shoulder. "Spicy garlic chicken."

"My lucky night." He paused. "Everything okay?"

"It will be." She turned then and sighed, the spoon dripping sauce on the floor. "Stephanie had the baby, and I went to see her, but of course Trey answered the door. I *wanted* to see her, but not him. I'm such an idiot to think he wouldn't be there."

He calmly took the spoon and set it on the counter. "You're not an idiot. You're making an effort to recover a valued friendship. So is she, and Trey is just part of the picture."

"I understand, but realize that for me, this is extremely uncomfortable."

"I do understand, I think."

"He doesn't like it either, and I get that, too."

"Anna, who does like it when a relationship doesn't work out?"

She changed the subject. He could hardly fault her. He understood fully why she didn't want to have children with Trey once she realized his true interest was elsewhere, but Chris had never asked if she wanted children. She hadn't asked him, either.

"What happened today? You look tense yourself." She regarded him with insightful contemplation.

"I'm processing."

"A typical non-answer."

"I'm not being evasive, I just don't have any real information."

He was still trying to decide how to handle it. He could show Loretta and Kyle a picture of the quarry victim, but it was not very pleasant, and he doubted they'd ever seen Johnson. The house had already been sold by the time they decided to hide there.

163

Anna got a paper towel and wiped up the floor where the sauce had dripped. "I doubt my problem compares to yours. I knew they were having a baby, so no surprise there."

"No, I suppose not, but it bothers you."

"Some," she admitted. "I think I'm past it, and then I figure out I'm not quite there."

"Falling out of love must be harder than falling in the other direction."

"Trey didn't seem to have any problem with it."

As reasonably as possible, he pointed out, "We can't all predict our futures, right?"

"No." The admission was reluctant. Anna turned away, a swing of dark hair shielding her expression. "He's a good-looking man who's intelligent and successful and gets what he wants accomplished. So are you."

Was she comparing them or giving him a compliment? It was hard to be sure. He stood there, not knowing what to say at first. "I certainly don't pretend to know his mind, but my impression is he would never intentionally hurt you. He doesn't seem like that sort of man."

"I agree; he doesn't."

That statement still left him in the dark as to how to respond. So he changed the subject. He didn't normally talk about cases, but this was relevant, given the circumstances. "We have a homicide victim connected to the Ivy House."

That changed her focus. "You do?"

"Yes. This is a very strange case. If those walls could talk, I believe they would have a lot to say. It would sure as hell make my job easier."

"Your job will never be easy." It was her turn to slant the topic back in a different direction. "Do you ever want children? I see you with Chloe, and so I wonder, but I've never asked."

And she was thinking about her ex-husband now as a father.

So much for not asking.

Answering this seemed like dangerous ground. "I suppose I've always assumed that, in the natural course of things, if I got married it would happen if we mutually agreed it should." Chris kept his tone neutral. "What about you?"

"With the right man, yes."

He had the uncomfortable feeling she was fighting tears. He understood why but was helpless to fix this particular problem. Anna was a strong individual, that he did know, but everyone had weak moments now and then.

It was a diplomatic issue if there ever was one. He was probably leaving, and she knew it. The FBI hadn't given a green light quite yet, so he was still in limbo, and was well aware the process took a long time, so all he could do was wait. Federal law enforcement was different from what he did now, so the future was uncertain.

At this moment anyway, he was not the right man.

"I agree, if I could have a Chloe to greet me with smiles and hugs every night when I came home, that would be a positive in a sometimes negative world."

"I agree with that as well." Her smile was a little wobbly, but at least no tears fell. "She seems to have become quite attached to you."

"I live with the moppet; that's my allure."

Anna shook her head. "Even at her age, she knows you're a nice man helping her mommy and daddy."

"Some help." He walked over and took a beer out of the refrigerator. "I haven't linked anything together yet. Maybe as evidence rolls in, we'll be able to see if this pieces together."

"I believe sharing your home is giving help."

He shrugged. "I wasn't using that bedroom anyway, I go to the cabin every chance I get, and otherwise I'm working."

His phone pinged and he took it out and glanced at the screen. A message from Carter. *You might want to come back to the office and look at the ME's report. It just came in. Lawrence wants a quick meeting.*

His point had just been made. "I've got to go back to work."

Anna took it in her stride. "If you do, you do. I'll make you a plate."

An understanding woman was like gold, he decided as he drove back. Since they seemed to be currently living together, it was a good thing. Not alone together, by any means, since there were three extra people involved, but Anna slept next to him each night.

Lawrence and Carter were waiting for him. Doreen was at her desk, but Chris wasn't sure she ever left it, so that wasn't surprising. She just pointed at the office with a pen. "There you go, sweetheart. Have fun."

Lawrence never lost any time. "Sit down and let's go through this fast. Read the report, so we're all on the same page before we start this shindig."

Chris scanned through it. Cause of death on the unidentified victim was blunt force trauma to the skull. Manner of death, probably homicide.

"Well, hell," he muttered.

Carter said, "Why kill a man and store him in a basement? And then murder the realtor of the same house?"

Lawrence looked distinctly unhappy. "Obviously something was going on under our noses."

"It wasn't a secret that it was an empty structure, or I wouldn't have my current houseguests. But they didn't move in until after the place had been sold, so they can't answer our questions. It was just a temporary hiding place."

"This Lattrell that got the kid in trouble in the first place, any luck on that angle?" Lawrence was focused, but he was like that all the time.

Unfortunately, the answer was not yet confirmed. "Loren thinks it might be George Riley."

"Are you serious?"

"That was his guess. If it is or isn't, the man was using an alias when he persuaded Kyle to break the law for some easy money and said he was law enforcement." Chris had to add, "Maybe he *is* our dead guy in the basement."

It had occurred to him that the not yet positively unidentified man could be the one who'd approached Kyle, but that would make him a suspect. If shown a picture, either way, guilty or innocent, he should say no. He was not a stupid young man, even if he'd made a questionable decision.

Clearly, Carter was following the same logic. "You can ask, but if Kyle identifies the guy, it really gives him a forerunner spot as the only person with a motive and opportunity, and we still won't know who the victim really is."

"You're operating on location." Chris had an argument.

"I'm operating on opportunity."

The sheriff stopped the debate. "I think that kid drove a truck with a load of pot a time or two for some extra cash, and that's his biggest sin." Lawrence rubbed his jaw. "If the dead man is George Riley and his partner in crime, then I'm guessing we have a small drug war going on. They were moving the stuff, and it was infringing on someone else's business. Damn, this battle makes me tired. Even if the state made it legal, I doubt it would change anything between the growers and dealers. It might be worse. If it was this Lattrell aka George Riley in that basement, we can figure that out easy enough. If it isn't Riley, someone probably has reported our victim missing under a different name. Work that. I want to know who he is and why he was killed."

Meeting over. Lawrence usually handled it that way. Said his piece, and he was done and just walked out.

"Easier said than done," Carter observed as he left. "No ID, no missing person report on Riley, and I doubt he looks a whole lot like he did in life, after being dead for a while. Loren could be wrong."

"I'll show the picture from the morgue to Kyle and see what he says about it being Lattrell." It was the best Chris could do. If the sample they took from the foyer matched Johnson's blood, Kyle really could be in trouble. He had obvious motive to kill both of them. It could be argued one had gotten him into a bad situation, and the other was entering a building where he was sheltering his family.

Why would Johnson go there when the house was already sold?

If that was even his blood. The DNA results would tell the tale, but that was a significant unanswered question.

They walked out together to blue skies, but there were monolith clouds building in the distance indicating impeding thunderstorms. Carter looked reflective. "Trouble on the horizon."

Chris agreed. "That's the truth, and I'm not talking about the weather. Lawrence is unhappy with the body count in this county lately, and I am too."

"You haven't heard from your favorite caller recently, have you?"

"No."

"Makes me wonder if he's dead."

"Or just enjoying the game."

CHAPTER TWENTY-ONE

The war was fought on two sides, of course. That's what constitutes a dispute that cannot be resolved except with a determination to eliminate your enemy. Vanquish is not an adequate word.

Eliminate is more appropriate.

Having a focused purpose was the key.

The resulting bloodbath proved both sides believed that with a purpose.

* * *

There were roses on her desk. Quite a spray too, at least a dozen long-stemmed, beautiful, full-crimson blooms.

Whitney looked, but there was no card.

"I accepted them for you, since you were out of the office." Will Beeson looked amused at her expression standing in the doorway of her office. "Mr. Waylan is apparently not just interested in your skills as an architect, but I knew that already."

The assumption was probably correct. It had to be Ross. It was a nice romantic gesture and, considering what he'd said to her recently, maybe not surprising. He didn't want to talk about it, but this was a statement anyway. She admitted, "We're seeing each other."

All of each other, she could have added, *sans clothing*, but she had a feeling Will Beeson already knew that their relationship went beyond just friendship.

"I sensed a rather serious attraction." Will's smile was benign.

"Time will tell how serious."

"I suppose that's a sensible way to look at it. How's the house coming along?"

The basement was still off limits, and as far as she knew, all work was suspended at this time, so that was a hard question to answer. She had no idea if Cal or Ross wanted anyone to know about the body in the basement, but it was hardly a state secret, since the construction crew all knew. "I don't know how to describe the progress. There have been a few glitches already, but I suppose that is to be expected with any major renovation."

"I'm sure it is, but we're part of the planning, not the execution."

He was correct there, but she thought that no one really expected a hidden dead man to be the problem. Her response was neutral. "It's all being handled as best as possible, I'm sure."

By the police. She didn't add that part. Once again, she wasn't positive she should say anything.

"Keep me posted."

He left, and she sat and looked at the flowers, debating whether to call and thank Ross or wait until later, because it seemed like they saw each other every evening now. Besides, he was at work.

She compromised and sent him a text instead. *Thank you so much for the gorgeous roses.*

Maybe a minute later, he called her. "Whitney, I'd love to take credit for it, but I did not send you flowers."

That made her blink and think out loud. "Oh. Then who did?"

"You tell me."

"I have no idea. There was no card. I obviously assumed you."

"I don't want to sound like a jealous lover, but I don't like it."

She didn't either. "I really can't think of anyone else who would send me expensive roses like the ones I'm looking at right now."

"No ex-boyfriend? Not someone who's asked you out and you turned them down?"

Whitney thought it over. "To be honest, no one comes to mind. This is strange."

"Maybe someone's sending me and Cal a message."

That was an interesting supposition. "Because of the house?"

"Well, sweetheart, think about it. This all seems to center around the house. You are Cal's sister, and I'm involved with you, and you are the architect. We have a bloody mess without an explanation and a dead body. Maybe they're indicating they don't like our idea of developing the property."

That hadn't occurred to her.

"By sending me flowers?"

"Hard to tell. They could be pointing out that you matter to both of us, and they're aware of it."

"You don't know that." But that was a disturbing theory.

"I know I didn't send you flowers, but someone did, and the omission of a card bothers me."

That was a valid point. Suddenly the blood-red roses weren't quite as lovely. Ross was not a detective, but he was a smart man with a quick mind.

"That kind of speculation bothers me," she said, "but you can hardly call the sheriff's office and complain about a flower delivery to your architect."

"Yes, I can." There was grim determination in his tone. "I think Detective Bailey will be interested in anything out of the ordinary. I'm going to let him know, and he can decide if he thinks it means anything."

She couldn't see how a detective would be interested in a mysterious floral gift, but maybe Ross was right. It was unusual, but it was possible the florist just forgot to put the card with it. People made mistakes all the time.

"I don't even know what florist the bouquet is from. I was out of the office when it was delivered."

"There can't be all that many around here. I bet it would be easy enough to find out. When we hang up, I'm calling Bailey. I'd lay odds Cal would agree with me."

It was hard to believe that someone would send flowers as a word of warning, but then again, the recent bizarre events were hard to believe too. "If you're determined to call Bailey, let me know what the detective thinks if you believe that's a reasonable course of action."

"I do. What are we doing tonight? I'm not leaving you alone. My house or yours? It's your choice."

The assumption might have annoyed her with anyone else, but she'd assumed, too, that they'd spend the evening together. "Mine. I'll make dinner."

"I'll take that, since you're better at it than I am."

"I guess I'll see you later."

She got up then and went to Will's office, to ask if maybe he'd noticed a logo on the delivery vehicle of the person who delivered the flowers, but he was on the phone. And though she was puzzled over who might send them, she was hardly convinced they were some sort of ominous message.

So she left the question unasked and went back to work.

* * *

The stately building was becoming familiar territory. Framed by trees, it had a faded elegance like an aging southern belle.

Now I'm getting poetic, Chris thought wryly.

"Why are we doing this again?"

He looked at Carter as they got out of the car. "The unusual interest in the house means something. I don't want to miss the connection. We always look at the people, but I think the catalyst is the location in this case."

"Whatever it was, Johnson was part of it."

"Hell yes, he was. I've been trying to guess why he'd go back to a property he'd already sold and closed on, and can't think of a reason he would trespass, other than he already had keys and was coming to retrieve something he knew was here."

"Or meet someone here, because he knew no one was living on the property yet."

"Bad decision, if that's the case. The question is, who?"

The front porch had been repaired, he saw, but not replaced, probably just enough to let the construction workers safely cross it. At least they wouldn't break a leg just going in. He tried to picture Loretta carrying Chloe into the house across that rickety mess and felt a pang of acute relief nothing bad had happened.

He was becoming quite fond of that child. Soon she'd be moving on, and he was all for her parents repairing their lives, but he had a feeling he and the moppet were going to really miss her.

The front door was unlocked as Waylan and Nolte had promised, so they just walked on in without a warrant. It wasn't like they were looking to arrest anyone. They were just going to search the house.

For what, was the real question.

Old rooms, some with tools scattered about. The kitchen was definitely torn apart, but the basement was unfortunately their goal. "If I wanted to hide anything, it would be down there," Chris pointed out.

"I wish it wasn't true." Carter eyed the staircase with open distaste. "Dark cellars aren't my favorite."

"That's my point. They aren't anyone's favorite, so a good place to hide something."

"I agree. I just don't like it."

"Buck up, because we're going down there." Chris took out his flashlight. "I'm hoping for no spiders myself. I can handle just about anything else, but I do not like spiders."

"Well, buck up yourself." Carter sounded amused. "I'm going to lay odds there are a few down there."

He was pretty sure there were too, but they needed to figure this out. He flicked on the flashlight. "No more corpses and I'll be fine. Who the hell has an organ in their basement?"

"Small organs were a thing at one time. I think my grandmother had one."

The steps were narrow and steep, and yes, laden with cobwebs, which Chris ignored. It smelled damp and musty, not surprising considering the age of the house. The floor was not poured concrete but packed dirt, which had, over the years, become a solid surface. It had clearly also become a storage space for discarded items. The mess was clearly not something the family had wanted to face before they sold the property. His light raked across a jumble of broken furniture, boxes, and rusted appliances. "No wonder no one wanted to sort through all of this."

Carter muttered, "I know I don't, but if you're so convinced there's something to be found here, let's do it."

They began a meticulous search, and it wasn't easy to do without better lighting, but he knew the house played into murder — not for the first time in its history — and the two recent ones meant something.

"There's something here."

He found it by accident, actually. Two big crates in a remote dank corner. He flipped over the lid of one and then the other. They were both full of guns.

"Carter. What the hell? Over here."

Not just guns but weapons he didn't particularly recognize, and he was a police officer.

His partner was equally mystified. "It looks like an arsenal."

"What are they?"

"Antique." Carter took one out and examined it very carefully. "These are fairly old. I hope this thing isn't loaded and doesn't blow my hand off or something."

"Civil war?" It was a guess, since Chris wasn't an expert on old guns; still, he'd seen pictures. "If so, they'd be worth a fortune, at a guess."

"Two whole boxes of them? How is that possible?"

"I don't know. Taken from dead or captured soldiers?"

"Surely not."

"Carter, it was a war. Both sides were desperate. If you took the fallen enemy's weapon, it only made sense."

His partner just looked at him. "How did so many of them end up here?"

"That's a good question. We need someone who can date them with more certainty."

"Do Waylan or Nolte know these weapons are here?"

"I doubt it, but someone does."

"Two deaths over a treasure trove of old guns, that's your theory?"

It was actually, now that they'd found them. "If they really are worth a lot of money, then yes, 'theory' is an accurate word. As a motive for murder, monetary gain frequently comes into play."

"I agree. But we have to figure out who."

"The antiquities market is widespread," he muttered. "These guns are worth money, if they are what I think they are."

There was no question Carter was pragmatic. "We're still left without even a suspect."

"I'd suspect Johnson, if he wasn't dead. You can't tell me he didn't come down here to measure and take a look around."

"Then he never listed the property." Carter was getting on board with it.

Chris pointed out, "Why not use it yourself? The perfect storage unit. No one asking questions, and no one else finding the contraband as you sell it on the black market to private collectors and take the money."

"Someone figured it out."

"And took over the business? Maybe. Let's keep looking."

They thoroughly covered the space — and yes, there were some more spiders — but found nothing else that might explain why two men were murdered.

Once they were back in the car, it was quiet, both of them thinking. Carter was driving, and Chris was the one that broke the silence. "Johnson told someone. He wasn't married, so maybe someone he worked with, or a friend?"

"Girlfriend who mentioned it to the wrong person?"

"Stranger things have happened."

"At least we have some sort of lead to pursue."

His phone rang then. He looked at the display and answered immediately. "This is Bailey."

CHAPTER TWENTY-TWO

I was never sure if I believed in heaven or hell. As events unfolded, I think the conclusion was that they both happened when we were on earth, not in the obscure place we ultimately were going.

Heaven was blue eyes and silky hair and soft lips.

Hell was the fallout from my obsession with heaven.

I started something I couldn't finish and many people paid the price.

* * *

There was thunder in the distance and a brief flash of lightning. He barely noticed, because the book was more than interesting, but the atmosphere suited the disquieting content.

Last man standing seemed to be the theme. A fight to the end.

A stubborn competition gone wrong, all started by one man's passion for a woman he couldn't have.

Ross was lucky in that he had a passion for a woman he *did* have. Or thought he did. It wasn't like Whitney had said anything, but she had slept in his arms every night since the first night they'd made love.

It was a new perspective for him. Sex had involved tran-sient pleasure before this experience, but making love was different. Emotion was involved; he was trying to define new territory.

"Storm coming. You can't sleep?"

He glanced up to see Whitney, disheveled but lovely, come into the living room. She looked sleepy; maybe the rumbling and flashes of light had woken her. "Just reading about the history of the infamous battle of the Maddox clan with the Wheatleys. Pretty bloodthirsty stuff."

"Tell me about it?" She was wearing a thin silk cami-sole and plaid shorts, and looked like a college girl with her tumbled fair hair and bare legs and arms. At twenty-six, she wasn't all that far past university age, but he now knew her body well, and she was definitely a woman, not a girl.

He said, "It's a perspective I would never have chosen — a ghost tells the story, essentially. I'm finding it compelling, though."

"Compelling? A powerful word. I've already told you I want to read it." She sank into a chair opposite and crossed her elegant legs in a graceful movement that most certainly caught his attention.

Focus on the topic. "I want to know who sent it to me."

"I have an idea."

"Will Beeson?"

She lifted a brow. "I see we're thinking along the same lines. He's just the type of man who might do something like that. I think I'd label him as intelligent, but a bit eccentric. I could see him sending it to you."

He didn't disagree. "If it was him, I find it odd he never mentioned it to me. Then again, maybe he's enjoying having an influence on this project from a distance?"

"He's very interested in buildings, as you know, and the historical aspect intrigues him."

Ross tapped the book. "It's interesting that Beth Garret can't find information on the author."

"If anyone could, she could." Whitney looked reflective. "Her and Cal? I find that an odd combination, but who knows?"

"Who does? Look at us."

"I'm not your kind of girl?" Her smile was teasing.

"I believe you're exactly my kind of girl." He smiled back wryly. "I was at least smart enough to know Cal would warn me off, so I kept my distance as best I could."

"The book is a ghost story?" She looked intrigued and let that comment go.

"I don't know if I'd call it that. But it's told by a dead man. It's a unique approach, since his death set off the events that caused quite a few more casualties on both sides. The quarrel was over a woman. That's not a new story."

"Are there *any* new stories?" She frowned. "So the author has him telling the tale because he was killed by his rival for her . . . affection? I don't how else to put it."

"In our house. Knife to the chest. Straight-out murder."

"Disturbing, I guess that would the word."

"Quite a bit of drama ensued. People killed each other, and some were hanged for their crimes." He paused, then added, "Cal and I had no idea when we bought it. Beautiful old house with good bones we could buy for almost nothing. As an investment, it seemed simple enough."

"But a body in the basement is just not simple at all."

He couldn't agree more. "No. At least the police don't seem to think we put it there."

"That would be stupid of you both, and I think it's obvious to anyone you aren't. Neither you nor Cal. To bring in a crew that might find it? No. Besides, there are plenty of places in this neck of the woods to hide a body. Why would you choose your own cellar?"

There was a certain logic to that, and besides, he didn't recognize the man at all, so tying them together would be difficult. "I wouldn't, because I wouldn't kill anyone in the first place. Unless, I suppose, they threatened someone I love." *Like you.* He didn't say it out loud. He wasn't quite comfortable with it yet.

"I wouldn't either, but someone put that body there."

"I'm counting on Detectives Bailey and Carter to find out who he is and who did it because that's out of my area of expertise."

"No, you just build Cursed Castles."

"For the record, you designed it, and Cal is building it. I just did the legwork."

"You made it happen. It was your idea once he'd found the property; my brother told me that flat out."

Hopefully it was a good one but now he wasn't as sure.

* * *

Ross was a complex man and Whitney was still learning her way around the maze. He was intelligent and passionate, but also cautious emotionally. They were figuring each other out as they went along without talking too much about it.

"I believe it's an excellent idea." She was cautious too but had taken a leap and didn't feel it was a mistake.

"I hope so, since you're part of the project."

"How could anyone possibly predict what's happened?" She tried to sound reasonable; it *was* a reasonable question.

"I know I didn't," he admitted, running fingers through his already rumpled hair. "Mysterious tenants, bloody handprints and a dead body in the basement, an old, deadly feud haunting the house . . . it sounds like a Gothic novel."

She had to agree. "I still think the history will appeal to people."

"Well, let's hope so. We're on this road headed somewhere."

That remark could have a double meaning. "We could be," she responded softly.

He looked at her. "It's up to you. I'm trying to let you figure out how you feel about it."

Was he referring to the house or to them? "I'm doing the same for you."

"Whitney, I think I've made a more definitive statement of my feelings than you have."

Definitely them.

"I've slept with you." She looked back directly. "Never anyone else before, only you. How definitive is that?"

It took a moment, but he said quietly, "Very. I think this is a new kind of relationship for both of us."

She didn't know what he wanted and wasn't sure she did either. Was she falling in love with him? Oh yes, that was a given. If she had to call it — and listened to her brother — she would be far from the first, which wasn't a surprise. Attractive, intelligent, personable men were hard to find in her opinion, and that was why she was still single and had chosen to wait, hoping for the right one. Had she found him? Only if he felt he had found her too.

Her phone pinged from its place on the coffee table.

"At this time?" Ross asked, glancing at the clock over the mantel. "It's almost midnight. Who would text you now?"

She got up and rushed to look, alarmed because of the hour. To her relief, she saw the name and number. "Beth is a night owl; trust me, I know from when I lived with her. I don't think she ever notes the time."

Quickly, she scanned the message, then she glanced up. "I think it's really for you more than me. She's figured out who wrote the book and asked me to tell you his real name wasn't Richard Gothard, it was Richard Maddox. Like from one of the families involved."

"How did she find out?"

"Well, the message starts with: *I have a friend at the Library of Congress who came through.*"

"Okay, that's very interesting. So the person who wrote that book lived in our house, or is a descendant anyway."

"The Maddox family once owned the house?" She was unaware of that part of the story.

"Yes, they did. And it's a start anyway. I owe her for trying so hard and coming through."

"Beth is great. A bit bookish, but that hardly means boring. She's just off in her own world half the time."

"That puts an interesting slant on this whole thing." He pointed at the book. "So, if a relative wrote it, maybe that's why he did it from the point of view of one of the victims."

"It's not quite the usual way to write a book, I agree."

"I wonder who sold the house to the couple who gave it to the bank. There's more backstory there."

"Someone along the way inherited it."

"And didn't want it, or lived so far away it wasn't practical. There are quite a few reasons why it might be sold. I'd like to learn more about Richard Maddox. I think it will only help promote the hotel."

She felt a twinge of humor. "You really are a money guy, aren't you?"

It was his turn to look amused. "That's why I went for a degree in business."

And he'd also gotten a master's degree at Vanderbilt, which might be in Tennessee but was a prestigious university. He'd been able to enter into his ambitious venture for a reason.

"I'm impressed with the vision. That everything hasn't gone according to plan isn't surprising. That's life." She was serious.

"And death, apparently."

"I think it works that way."

"Now you're a philosopher?"

"Not by choice but by circumstance." She was only half joking.

He stood, extending his hand. "Let's go back to bed?"

Lightning flashed in the background, jagged spikes against the night sky visible through the picture window.

She said, "I don't like these summer storms." He could hardly do anything about the forces of nature, but she'd feel better if he was next to her, whether it was logical or not.

Strong arms, a muscular chest, and his breathing in the dark . . . she was getting used to the intimacy.

"It'll pass."

"I know. But sleeping with you is better, whatever the weather."

It was interesting that the intimacy she'd avoided until now just felt right. There was no doubt the wind was picking up; she could hear it. The warm clasp of his hand was very welcome.

"I'm glad you feel that way."

He wanted her to say it — she felt it — but she wasn't ready yet. She'd trusted him enough already and didn't regret it, but truth be told, an inner voice whispered to her that telling him she was in love with him might just make him walk away. That he'd said it was no guarantee of permanence.

When they reached the bedroom, he pulled her into his arms and whispered against her mouth, "I know it's late, but I want you again."

At that point, she decided she'd worry about permanence later.

CHAPTER TWENTY-THREE

The thirst for revenge leaves a raw throat and an unsatisfied soul. I believe my father found that out the hard way. An eye for an eye and a tooth for a tooth might be biblical, but the result is murder.

I know all about that first-hand.

There are certain doors that just should not be opened.

* * *

Kyle stared at the picture. "That's him. Lattrell is . . . dead?"

Chris said, "I'm afraid so, if you're positively identifying him."

"Well, that's the man that asked me if I wanted to make some decent money under the table." Kyle went restively to the refrigerator and got out a beer. "God, I think that tells me I was smart to hide Loretta and our daughter. I hated making them live that way, but I was scared to death those were serious threats."

"But you aren't getting them now."

"No, but then again, I quit doing it and I'm only working a short schedule. I noticed Lattrell wasn't around for weeks at least." He took a compulsive drink. "I'm also staying here. They made their point, and I understood they were serious. I think they realize that, and I also think these guys don't want to show up on your watch. Or, at least, I'm counting on that."

It was his policy to never reveal information on open cases, otherwise he might have pointed out the location of the body implicated the young man drinking beer in his kitchen, but he didn't really think he was a prime suspect. "So the man you knew as Lattrell worked for your company?"

"No, he was an independent contractor that delivered supplies. I usually checked them in and unloaded the truck."

Quite often his job wasn't easy, but Chris wasn't thrilled with this puzzle. "Surely your boss could identify him."

"I don't know. I think he did business over the phone with Lattrell's employer. I just listened to the project supervisor and did my job."

"Well, you've at least confirmed how he might fit into this."

"I wish I could tell you more."

What he had told Chris was confirmation that he probably hadn't killed his partner in crime, because if he knew where the body was, he'd never had done the identification. That was something, anyway, though Carter might argue it. The opportunity was certainly there and the location damning, but as young as Kyle may be, he was smart enough to make the connection. That he didn't indicated he did not know where the body had been found.

Johnson had, if Chris was a betting man. Maybe he was the killer, or maybe he'd been meeting the killer, now that the house was sold, so they could remove the body. Then the guilty party felt Johnson knew too much, so he killed Johnson instead, and got rid of Johnson but left Lattrell?

Hard to say. Moving a body up steep old stairs was not all that easy alone. Maybe the killer felt like he wasn't easily linked to Lattrell unless Johnson had told someone. He certainly moved *that* man's body, but maybe that killing had been more premeditated. Lattrell's killer arranged a meeting with Johnson, ostensibly to move the body, but had a different agenda. He'd brought a tarp and a vehicle, to make disposal easier.

Why did he leave the knife in Chris's cabin? Most murderers wouldn't. Symbolic in some way? And those guns . . . he thought they had something to do with it, but he was having a hard time trying to piece it all together. If they were worth a lot of money, then there was certainly motivation.

He needed to figure it out.

Easier said than done.

He texted Carter. *We have identification.*

His partner called him immediately. "Do we?"

"He was the other carrier."

"So drug crime after all."

"I don't think so, for Johnson. We just have to connect the two murders."

"Lawrence will be disappointed we aren't solving his problem, if you're right." Carter was the king of equanimity. "So let's treat this problem by solving a different equation. Who killed these two men and why?"

"I'm strongly inclined to think it's the house."

"A house killed two people?"

"No, somehow the history of a house killed two people."

"I've got admit I'm not following your logic on this one. Lattrell, or Riley, or whatever his real name is, was into transporting items for the right price. Maybe he moved those guns there, since Johnson was already letting someone use the property illegally."

"Or maybe someone knew they were there, and killed Lattrell because he found them, and then Johnson because he sold the property and was no longer of any use. In fact, he was a liability, because he knew what they were doing."

"Who would that be?"

"Good question." Unfortunately, he didn't have the answer. No suspects in their line of vision.

Except maybe one.

"I might have an idea. I'll let you know if I think we should follow up."

In the meantime, he needed to figure out who Lattrell might be besides a dead man in a basement. He knew thanks to Loren it was probably Riley using a false name. He needed to prove it with DNA.

How was the question.

He hadn't been reported missing, so his employer was the only lead.

"You do better with the professionals. Go talk to this construction boss? If he is an independent contractor, that man had to find him somewhere. I just want to make sure we have the right victim. A visual identification is a good start, but who is he, really? I'll do research. Facial recognition might help us if he's ever been arrested, but that's dicey with decay as a factor."

"Well, you navigate the computer better than I do." Carter was as pragmatic as ever. "I'll take care of the interview if you'll send me the information. Kyle recognized him and so did Dr Loren, so maybe the system will too."

"I will."

They did have different skill sets, true. Usually it worked, because there was a balance between a conservative approach and a more liberal way of handling things. Chris had to admit he was more of a shoot-from-the-hip kind of law enforcement officer, and his partner followed protocol like it was his religion.

The note was on his desk.

Doreen's handwriting.

I think we are coming around full circle.

He went straight to her desk. "Same guy?"

"Sounded like him." She glanced up from her computer. "What it means, I have no idea. I took your message, and now you get to figure it out, lover boy."

Not as easy as it sounded.

"Lover boy? Carter told me about the bet, by the way."

She looked predictably unrepentant. "Be happy you have an interesting personal life. You're currently sleeping with the ex-wife of a prominent defense attorney and harboring the family of a drug runner, not to mention getting mysterious messages from an unknown source. Without you, I'd be stuck watching soap operas."

How the hell she knew all of that was a mystery, but he'd already discerned Doreen had mystical powers.

So he just let it go and said dryly, "Thanks."

He went back to his desk and scanned in the unattractive picture from the morgue and gave the recognition software a try.

* * *

It wasn't like Ross regularly dropped by her office, but he took off a little early and did it anyway. Whitney was at her desk and looked surprised when he walked in, but her lips curved in a welcoming smile. "Hello. I thought you had a really busy day."

"I did. Thought I'd stop by to see you instead of the usual phone call. No new flower deliveries?"

"No."

"No more phone calls?"

"No."

That made him relax at least a little, and suddenly he noticed the shining fall of her hair, moving across her shoulders as she shook her head. He really was in love with her. It was still unsettling every time he acknowledged it, but he was getting used to the idea; he just wasn't sure what to do about it. Maybe both his sister and Cal were right, and commitment scared the hell out of him.

"I was just concerned," he said, a bit belatedly.

It won him another smile. "You're worried about me?"

"Of course."

"Then kiss me, and we'll talk about this over a glass of wine later."

Kiss me? He didn't have to be asked twice. "That's a date."

They shared a nice long kiss, and then he let her go. "Ask Beeson if I can talk to him again."

"You want to ask him about the book?" Her aquamarine eyes looked right through him.

"Whitney, he knew the title cold. Beth even had problems making a connection to the author. He didn't. I don't have any idea what's going on, but maybe he does."

It took a moment, but she admitted, "He did say he wanted to be kept up on the project."

"That sounds like a perfect excuse to meet with him. Anyway, I want to ask him if he thinks there were transoms over the doors at one time that could possibly be replaced. A genuine historical question."

"A good start, but he's a smart man. He'll know you're fishing for other answers."

"I want him to know I'm fishing for those answers. And I'd like to think I'm also a smart man."

He wanted to tell her last night, as he'd lain in bed, that he'd wondered if maybe Beeson had bought her those flowers. True, he was twenty years older at least, but it happened often enough that a man became enamored with a much younger woman. She'd been previously uninvolved, and suddenly she had a love interest.

Was that new dynamic a catalyst for Beeson's interest in the house?

Maybe it was.

"He was the one who suggested I'd sent the flowers?"

The shift in conversation obviously threw her off. Whitney took a moment. "Yes. Why?"

"I'm revising my original theory that the flowers were symbolic, because whoever killed two people isn't subtle enough for that."

She wasn't slow on the uptake. "You think *Will* bought me those flowers?"

"I think it's possible there was a romantic gesture involved, yes."

"Then why would he imply it was you?"

"Because he knew you'd thank me, and I'd tell you it wasn't me."

"What would be the point of that?"

"I think that he's letting you know there's another interested party."

"Ross, he's decades older—"

He held up his hand to interrupt. "His interest doesn't stun me. After all, *I'm* interested. He's not really old enough for it to be surprising."

He could tell it hadn't occurred to her. She sat back, her expression disconcerted. "He's never said or done anything to indicate that you're right."

"I don't know I'm right. But I might be. Maybe all he wanted was to give you beautiful roses and enjoy your reaction to the gift. Men aren't all that complicated. A smile on a woman's face does a lot for us."

"Now you're a philosopher?" It was evident she didn't like his take on it.

"No, definitely not. But I've got some insight, I hope, being male and all."

"You are that. I can confirm it."

He had to smile. "I'm happy to say you can."

"Well, I'm hoping you're right about Will, since that's a lot easier to accept than someone sending them to me as a warning to you and Cal."

"I have to agree with you there." He meant it. If it was Beeson instead, that was harmless enough.

What wasn't harmless was the deep-seated feeling there was an unknown element of danger, and he had no idea where it was coming from.

"Young Mr Waylan." The tone was pleasant, and they both glanced up to see the subject of their conversation stop in the open doorway. He continued, "I guess I'm not surprised to see you here. How is everything coming on your ambitious project?"

It was just the phrasing and the way Beeson looked at him: Ross knew he wasn't wrong about the flowers. Well, good. The alternative was much worse, and he held the advantage — at least at the moment, though he doubted it endeared him to his opponent. "I wanted a few moments of your time, if you don't mind, since you're conveniently here. Can you spare them now?"

"For a minute or two, certainly." It was an affable response, but there was a certain wariness in the other man's eyes.

"The book, *Malice Aforethought*, how did you hear of it?"

"Ivy Manor is a historical home, so naturally when I heard about the book, I bought a copy, since it was once in my mother's family."

"How? My impression was that it's pretty rare." Ross was careful to keep his voice even as well. "I had a friend who's a librarian look into it."

"It might be, since it certainly is old, but I stumbled across a copy at a local bookstore."

That might be plausible enough. "I just wondered, since someone mailed me a copy, and it certainly is interesting." Then he let it go. "The original doors in the house would have had transoms over them, right?"

CHAPTER TWENTY-FOUR

A sense of place is important. I always thought so, but leaving it behind is not easy. I haunt these halls and empty rooms and have a sense of desolation because I can remember warm lights and laughter.

I'm not alone.

But I am lonely.

All of that was a long time ago. I've lost count of the years, since it doesn't really matter now, does it? If I knew, it wouldn't change anything.

* * *

Beautiful day. Blue skies and a warm wind blowing through the tops of the trees. The river was smooth and tame, which was unusual, though it depended on the rain. Chris tossed in a line and reclined in a camp chair as it drifted down into the water. Fishing wasn't so much a sport for him as it was a way to just sit and think.

He'd come to the conclusion that he was dealing with an amateur killer. He didn't believe any longer that it was organized crime. It was personal in both cases.

Conclusion two was the killer knew something about the history of the house, so he was local. By the time Chris was six years old, he'd heard about the infamous feud and the fatal stabbing that started it, but didn't really know the details, so the call to the location really hadn't registered at first. Waylan said someone had sent him a book about it, and the author appeared to be a descendant of one of the two warring families. A Maddox, in fact, using another name, so the story could be biased.

Then he mentioned the roses someone had just sent Ms. Nolte. On one hand, it could simply be an admirer, because she was worth looking at, but no note at all was kind of unusual. Chris didn't like it. Maybe she *was* at risk.

Carter would say he was being too analytical about motive and not enough about opportunity.

He would argue that motive helps you figure out what the opponent might do next.

In this case, he thought the killer was driven by impulse. Both murders showed a lack of control. There was no shared methodology, so the only thing that connected them was the location.

As he reflected over the scenic view of water and trees, he wondered again about the caller and what his purpose was, why he'd involved him in the first place.

Clearly Johnson had been killed well after Riley. Forensics had now established the identity of both victims. Neither one was in a grave, so what did the caller mean? He'd asked for the name of the victim at the time and gotten nothing.

Another victim?

That was a challenge he couldn't ignore. Directed at him, for whatever reason.

Cold case was his conclusion. He had at first thought it had something to do with the recent murders, but he wasn't sure about that any longer, except one of those was a copycat of a murder committed a century ago.

Not six feet deep.

It could refer to the body in the basement. Stored behind a musical instrument wasn't buried, but it could be construed that way.

His line tugged, and he was jolted out of his contemplation.

He'd deal with it later. Maybe he'd catch a nice fish and it would make his day.

Only his phone rang. A glance told him it was Anna. She sounded distressed when he answered. "Loretta called me. Kyle is missing."

So much for a quiet afternoon of contemplation. "Missing how?"

"He never went to work apparently and he's been very careful about that. Always shows up. Even when they were moving the marijuana, he did his regular job to make sure there was a steady income. No show, no call. His boss called Loretta to ask where he was."

He took that in as he landed a smallmouth bass, one that he would normally applaud. "When was he seen last?"

"I think at about seven this morning."

Well, *shit*. Late afternoon now . . .

He took the fish off the hook, cradling the phone between his ear and shoulder. "Let's not panic yet. Maybe he had a family emergency that his parents actually took the time to tell him about, or something happened he felt he needed to take care of right away."

"Please, Detective Bailey, don't tell me this doesn't give you pause, considering his partner in crime is dead and he'd been threatened."

He gently eased the fish back into the water, and it swam off. His reply was resigned. "It does. Let's see what I can do."

His contemplative, peaceful interlude with nature over, he went inside, collected the dog, and headed for his truck. What exactly he was going to do he wasn't sure, because a missing young man could be anywhere. For all he knew, Kyle could have caught a flight to Mexico to protect himself — and his family — from a new threat, but Chris wasn't sure that was the case. He would have thought, given where Kyle was living, he would have come to him or even the sheriff before running.

It wasn't good news for Chloe. At least Kyle seemed to genuinely care about his child, and she clearly adored him.

The problem was, finding a missing person wasn't the easiest task in the world, but maybe the man would do him a favor and just show up with a plausible explanation.

Or he'd departed for parts unknown, courtesy of someone with an agenda. Maybe, like Riley, he knew something important he didn't realize was a threat, or else they *thought* he might know it.

A classic damned if he does and damned if he doesn't.

All Kyle did was drive the truck carrying the product, according to him. Chris believed him, mostly because he thought he'd been honest so far — despite his transgression. He admitted it even knowing he could do jail time and had identified Lattrell.

Chris maybe went over the speed limit to get home.

Loretta met him at the door. She was pale and her cheeks were wet. "He won't answer his phone."

"We'll look for him, and there could be a simple explanation." He was hardly an expert at reassuring distraught young girls her age.

"He wouldn't do this. The only reason he did what he did was to support us when his hours got cut. He wouldn't risk losing his job."

The truth was, he agreed with her. "We can track his phone and look for his car as a first step. Is there anything else you can tell me?"

"I don't think so."

She looked so vulnerable. It took conscious effort for all law enforcement to distance themselves from the emotional part of the job, but he was involved in this now, on a personal level, especially with Chloe sitting on a small blanket in his living room building something with wooden blocks.

"Loretta, we will do our best to find him. Or he may pull in at any moment without us even looking."

Her mouth trembled. "I hope so."

He did too, since finding Kyle wasn't going to be easy if he was on the run. He highly doubted Kyle had a credit card, so tracing him that way wasn't viable. But he did have a cell phone, even if he wasn't answering. Best place to start.

At that point, *his* phone rang.

Lawrence. If the sheriff called, he answered. "Yes, sir?"

"Son, just when I think life can't get more complicated, it seems to do it anyway." Lawrence didn't sound annoyed, his tone more edgy than irritated. "Your young friend is here in my office, and he has a gun."

What? "Friend? Can you clarify?"

"The drug runner kid, Kyle."

Oh shit.

"I was just getting ready to look for him." Chris reached for his keys.

"Well, now you know where to find him."

"I'm on my way. Let me talk to Kyle. If he's on a ledge, I think I can talk him off it."

"No, no, I think you're not getting what I'm saying. The gun isn't pointed at me. I'm a lawman; I don't need you to rescue me, cowboy."

Well, that was a relief. Kyle didn't need any more trouble, but what the hell was going on? A gun?

"What kind of gun?"

"Old one. He says there are boxes of them."

A light dawned. Those Confederate pistols, Lattrell's body in storage, there in the old house where the weapons were kept . . .

Now there was a connection. Two murders and those valuable guns.

How did Kyle know about them? He implicated himself at every turn, but then again, Chris had just shown him the picture from the autopsy and never said where the body was found. What the heck was going on?

"I need to talk to him, right now. Keep him there, please, and I'll be there in a few minutes. I want a one-on-one and maybe I can break this case."

"I'll have Doreen sit on him."

Lawrence did occasionally have a sense of humor. Chris told Loretta, "Kyle is fine, and I know where he is, but I have to go. You and Chloe stay in, doors locked, got it?"

The relief in her expression was enough to make him think his job was sometimes worth it. Her voice quavered. "Got it."

"Anna will be here in a bit, but Kyle and I should be back soon, also."

Then he was out the door with a purpose, because he had some pointed questions that needed answering.

* * *

Anna hadn't expected a taxing day, but she'd had one, and was afraid of what might face her when she walked through the door. Instead, Loretta greeted her with a brilliant smile. "He's okay."

Young lovers. She wouldn't mind being one again, but in her case she'd been disillusioned by her first attempt. "What happened?"

"I don't know. Detective Bailey went to meet with him."

"He didn't tell you?"

"Does he tell you anything?"

Quite perceptive for a young woman. Anna had to be honest. "Actually, no, he really doesn't. I'm going to change into something more comfortable, and we can just wait. He always turns up, I just don't know when that will be."

"He does seem to come and go a bit, but that's his job, isn't it?"

That was certainly a discerning observation. He lived and breathed the job. It had cost him his last relationship; he'd admitted that. Anna was somewhat guilty of it too, so she understood. If she wasn't, why was she sitting in another person's home, with an adrift young woman and her toddler, instead of her own comfortable place?

Her mother would explain it was because she wanted to save the world.

Not true. She wouldn't lift a finger to help someone who threatened a child or a person who needed help, male or female. "I think he's married to his occupation, yes."

"He's nice." Loretta made a face. "Kyle's dad is so awful, and my father left my mother so long ago I don't remember him really. Just walked out the door. You're lucky."

Normally, when young girls like Loretta confided in her she didn't give out personal information. However, Anna made an exception. "Not so lucky. Yes, he's an exceptionally good man, but he's leaving for federal law enforcement. So I'm lucky only at the moment. Let me go change my clothes."

Just then, there was a knock at the door. With all that was going on, it gave her pause, but for all she knew, Chris was expecting a delivery or something, and being him, of course he didn't have a security camera. Anna turned. "I'll get that. You and Chloe stay back."

She opened the door to a young man with an affable smile and his hands in his pockets. He said, "Hi. Is Kyle here? I'm supposed to meet him."

"Meet him here?" She was suitably wary. Maybe she shouldn't have even answered the door, but then again, how could this person even know where Kyle was staying if he hadn't told him? However, in the course of doing her job, she'd learned a lot about reading people. She had the feeling that behind that smile he was lying to her.

"Yes. Can I come in maybe and wait for him?"

"Feel free to wait on the porch if you like." She was pleasant but firm.

"No, I think I'll come in."

He suddenly wrenched open the door. Anna stepped back so quickly she almost fell. He caught her wrist and jerked her upright, not gently. The smile was gone. "I'm going to have a few words with Kyle. Let's agree that you shouldn't interfere with it. He and I are old friends."

It wasn't like she hadn't dealt with angry men before. Interviews, visitations, courtrooms — you name it, she'd seen it. She stood her ground between him and Loretta and Chloe. "He *isn't* here."

"I can wait."

There was an interruption in the form of a cool, male voice. "Williams, take your hand off the lady and do it slow."

The tone was extremely effective.

Anna felt it shimmer through her and realized Chris had come through the back door, silent and unseen. Her knees felt weak, she was so relieved. No matter what, she would have stood between anyone and that child, but now she didn't have to.

Because she knew Chris would.

Her would-be assailant did let her go. But he didn't do it immediately, which was telling.

"Loretta, get her out of here." Anna used her voice that meant business, because this wasn't going to go well. She felt it. "Now."

Loretta had the sense to obey. There was a small cry of disappointment from Chloe at being removed from her blocks, but Loretta scooped her daughter up and left the room. The moppet was smart enough to follow.

"All I need to do is talk to Kyle." The young man tried the smile again.

It didn't work.

"About?" Chris's tone was implacable. "Maybe the reason you killed Riley? Yes, I'd already come to that conclusion."

"Who the hell is Riley, and why would you think I killed him?"

"I believe you knew him as Lattrell. You grow the product, and he moved it for you. I've talked to the DEA. You're on their radar, but who they really want are your distributors. Maybe you can make a plea, but if you killed Johnson too, I doubt it."

Dead silence. Anna wasn't sure just what was going on, but if it involved drugs, it wasn't good. She'd dealt with plenty of offenders and there was a dark side that emerged almost inevitably.

He moved one hand slightly toward his back. Chris said, with emphasis, "If you're reaching for a gun, don't do it. I promise you I'm faster and a better shot."

The chill that went down Anna's spine was very real, because if he was wrong, she was dead; she was a witness, and so was Loretta. Even little Chloe might be in danger. She didn't know the man, but evidently Chris did.

Afterward, she just stood there in shock, deafened by the sound of gunshots so close by, but Chris had been right. The young man was the one that went down, his weapon tumbling from his hand.

She barely heard Chris mutter a very profane word, and then say, "Some people just don't listen."

CHAPTER TWENTY-FIVE

Not to be morbid, but funerals are for the living, not the dead. There is no satisfaction for us, because we aren't invited. Just an observation born from experience.

* * *

Well, dammit.

How come nothing could be simple?

He'd told him flat out not to try it. At least he had a witness it was self-defense.

"Call Dispatch, please." Chris already prepared himself to surrender his weapon, but put it back for the moment. He held out his phone and pushed a button. "Tell Darlene there's a man down and give her the address."

Anna was nothing but stalwart, though pale. "I will."

Williams was still breathing, which was good, but he was sprawled in the living room, bleeding from his chest, gasping for breath. Chris knelt next to him.

Not good. Respiration sluggish, froth of blood on the mouth, so maybe a nicked lung. He could do the basics, but wasn't a medic.

"I warned him."

"I heard you." Anna was already back; calls to Darlene were short and sweet. "What can I do?"

"A towel to help stop the bleeding. I have to say, I really don't want him to die." He didn't need another fatal shooting pinned to his service record.

"I'll get one."

Together they did their best. Williams clearly couldn't talk, but he was alive, and it was a relief to finally hear the wail of sirens. Chris went to the door to wave them in and direct them to the location of their patient. Carter arrived not more than a minute later, of course, and Chris handed over his weapon. "He drew on me."

Carter nodded and took it with gloved hands. "I've felt like doing that once or twice. What's the story?"

"He showed up here wanting to talk to Kyle Sanders, but Sanders isn't here. Anna told him that, but he pushed past her and came in anyway. I saw the unfamiliar vehicle and came in through the back. He was confronting Anna and had his hand on her. I put an end to that, and then informed him I was well aware he grew weed, Kyle and Riley were moving it, and that he'd killed Riley. I think he saw the window shade going down on his life. So he reached for his piece, and that was a mistake."

Carter, who was wearing a lavender shirt that was quite the contrast to his usual crisp white, said, "Okay, so he was an idiot and has never seen *High Noon*."

"I didn't challenge him. I just told him not to do it."

"It seems like he should have taken that advice." Carter eyed them lifting the patient onto a gurney. "Let me talk to Anna and get her version, so you have backup in case he doesn't make it."

That was protocol, of course. "Loretta can also tell you he forced his way in." Since there was a witness, Chris was justified in self-defense, so he wasn't worried about that, but another shooting? "Kyle Sanders obviously knew about the guns, or he wouldn't have taken one to Lawrence. I suspect that's the only reason he's still alive, because Williams came here armed and probably ready to eliminate anyone who could testify against him."

"Drugs and guns are always a dangerous undertaking." They watched him being carried out.

"I can tell you he isn't the person who's been calling me and leaving messages with Doreen. That isn't his voice."

"So, what body is this person talking about? Johnson?"

"Well, Johnson wasn't six feet under, that's for sure. He was a floater." It was true. "Two different killers?"

Carter just shook his head.

"There's a connection," Chris said, "but I don't see it."

"I don't either. Let me talk to Anna and get our current problem cleared up so a report can be filed."

"Sounds good to—"

"What's happened?" The interruption was abrupt and frantic. Kyle burst in holding a grocery bag. "Why is there an ambulance pulling away?"

"A friend of yours dropped in." Chris gestured at his living room floor. "Loretta and Chloe are safe. Anna just went up there to check on them."

"Is that blood?"

"I'm afraid so. I thought you were right behind me." It was probably better for his life expectancy he wasn't. Chris merely said, "Be glad you weren't."

"I just stopped and got ice cream for Chloe. The store was busy . . . What friend?" Kyle looked truly confused. "No one knows I'm here."

"Frank Williams."

He seemed to genuinely think about it. "The neighbor to that old house? I don't know him except for him asking me what I was doing there one time."

Riley had been the main contact, so that might be true. Chris knew first-hand Williams kept a careful eye on the property and he'd have realized just who was camping out there. There were some unanswered questions, but Chris had not had the most pleasant afternoon. "Hand the ice cream to me and go see for yourself both of them are fine — and send Anna down. Detective Carter needs to talk to her."

Kyle gave him the bag and bolted for the stairs, and Chris remarked sardonically to Carter, "How the hell did I go from shooting someone in my own house to putting away ice cream for a toddler in roughly the space of an hour?"

"You do lead an interesting life."

"Well, I might get some ice cream later, so I do have something to think of that can improve my day. That is if Chloe will share."

He went and put it in the freezer and tried to not think about the ramifications of this afternoon's events. Another review, of course. That would be easy enough, but the FBI was not going to love it. Had there been a choice? No. Was there blood on his living room floor? Yes.

The man had barged in with a weapon, he reminded himself, and there had been three females at risk, one of them a child, plus it was self-defense; he'd acted when the intruder reached for his weapon.

End of story.

He doubted it. There would be press, and the other cases would come up. The office would back him, he knew that, but still . . .

All he'd wanted was a nice dinner and a quiet evening. Too much to ask? Apparently so.

He needed to call Lawrence, but the sheriff had probably already heard about it. Obviously, someone had contacted Carter. No doubt Anna had said that Chris wanted her to call it in and Darlene in Dispatch would tell Doreen, who would tell Lawrence he was involved.

Time for a beer. He was right by the refrigerator, so that was convenient, especially since he could hear that Anna had come downstairs. He twisted off the cap and contemplated how to clean up blood from the floor instead of thinking about if Williams was going make it. At the end of it all he figured philosophically the man had chosen his own path and might pay the ultimate price for it.

Did he think the young man had murdered at least one person? He did.

Two? He wasn't sure.

And then there was the possible third.

* * *

Anna answered the questions as calmly as possible and was grateful Detective Carter kept them short and to the point. At the end she *had* to add, "In my opinion, if it matters, I doubt I would be here to talk to you if it wasn't for Chris Bailey. I see disturbed people quite often. That man would have killed me, too, if I'd witnessed him shooting a law enforcement officer."

Carter seemed like a reasonable man. "I think you could be correct. I'll mention that you think he might have saved your life in my report."

"Maybe say I'm sure he did. That would be my opinion, not yours, but it's true."

"I'll take that into consideration."

When he left, she went into the kitchen to find Chris sitting at the table, drinking a beer and appearing very calm despite the grim afternoon. He looked up. "That was short and sweet."

"It wasn't a long story. My participation was only a few minutes. I think there's an open bottle of Chardonnay. I'll join you if you don't mind."

"Of course not."

She had to pause in the act of going to get a wineglass. "None of this bothers you?"

"All of this bothers me. I have a lot of unanswered questions, a bloody floor, a review now coming, and I don't like it. Beside all of that, there might be another killer out there and I don't have a handle on it."

But he was collected and cool, and she accepted the composure was just how he handled everything. "I can relate, to the extent every situation I deal with is stressful in some way. Not as drastic as yours this afternoon, but I deal with some very unhappy and desperate people."

"Speaking of which, I hope you realize I have some very pointed questions for Kyle that he's going to have to answer, but for now I just want to decompress. I say we order pizza for dinner, because you haven't had the easiest afternoon either after confronting the not-so-charming Mr Williams, witnessing a shooting, and then being questioned about it, so that you had to relive it. No need for you to cook for all of us."

"I'm fine with that."

"I'm going to finish this beer and then clean the floor." He grimaced. "My opinion is I didn't technically make the mess, our visitor did, but I suppose that point could be argued, and it is my house."

"And Chloe plays there. I promised I'd try to find them someplace else, and now that I think the threat is gone, it'll happen."

"I don't know if the threat is gone."

He sounded definitive enough it gave her pause. "Why?"

"Because while I think what happened with Riley was an argument over a drug deal that went south, why would our friend Frank stab a knife into the heart of the realtor who sold the property and dump him into a quarry?"

"He was ready to kill *you*." She had to point that out. "That decision just didn't go his way."

Chris looked like he was really thinking it over, musing out loud. "I don't see his motivation. The house was sold. It was a done deal. Maybe Johnson was there to help him move the guns, but those guns are still there. Both Carter and I saw them."

She had absolutely no knowledge of what he might be talking about. "What?"

"There's a cache of old guns in the cellar of that old house. I'm guessing the weapons are very valuable. Kyle told the sheriff that was where they picked up the weed to move it, so he and his unlawful associate stumbled over them. Now the associate is dead."

She digested this, sipping on her wine. "I'm starting to see the picture. It comes down to money."

"Unfortunately, most things do."

"Whereas you'd just as soon enjoy your simple cabin in the woods by the river?"

"You have that right. I'm a simple man."

No, he wasn't. Not by any means. "Chris, you are more complex than anyone I've ever met. So what do you think is happening?"

"There's another killer with a different agenda."

"Like what?"

"I'm trying to figure that out. This person that has been calling me and leaving messages, I don't get it . . . yet. But he's trying to lead me."

"I think you're right, but to what purpose?"

"You're the psychologist. You tell me."

"Whoever it is, is taunting you. It's a battle of the minds." She got up. "Finish your beer. I'll go clean the floor, and you get to order the pizza."

"No, I'll clean it up. I have hazmat on hand, and you know much better than I do what kind of pizza a toddler might eat." He got up, too, and intercepted her. "Anna, I'm sorry about this afternoon."

He was sorry? She'd brought it all to his doorstep, so in a certain way they were both to blame. "Like any of it was your fault."

"I involved you in the investigation."

"Good call, Detective. A child was at risk. I should have been involved." She meant it.

"Then you had to confront an angry killer and witness a shooting."

"So did you, because *I* brought everyone to your home."

And that's how Williams had found them. All he had to do was follow them because he was on careful surveillance of the property.

He smiled ruefully. "Fine, I don't think we need to argue over who is more responsible; we just need to accept the circumstances and move forward with our evening. I'll go get the kit and deal with the floor, and you can handle important pizza decisions."

She had to ask one question. "Did Kyle say why he didn't show up for work?"

"He said he went to work, but his supervisor is new and doesn't recognize him half the time, and he wasn't answering his phone because he forgot to charge it — which was why his boss called Loretta instead. He told me if I wanted to verify he was there, I could check his time card, because he punched in and out."

It was at least a plausible story.

"I don't see any reason you should check, because there was no crime; Loretta was just terrified something had happened to him. And he was evidently late because he went to see the sheriff and stopped for ice cream for his daughter."

"I agree, Anna. You don't have to convince me."

It saved his life, Anna was aware. She'd seen that potentially fatal confrontation, and Kyle was hardly a cool-headed, experienced law enforcement officer. He wasn't armed, either.

She knew it. She was just the lioness between her charges and anything that threatened them. "I know. Sorry. I advocate for anyone I think is vulnerable."

"That has registered with me." He looked faintly amused. "I'll go clean the floor."

CHAPTER TWENTY-SIX

When I was still able to enjoy it, I liked the outdoors. Deer moving in the fall, wild turkeys and the occasional prowling bobcat . . . life as I knew it. A simple country boy. Until I met her and everything changed. My obsession was my downfall, but not intentional. Had she not recip-rocated my feelings, I would have left it alone.

She is just as much to blame.

It is odd that, even now, I still love her.

* * *

Ross had sent Cal a message that the police wanted to talk to them once again.

He called back immediately. "About what? Tell me there isn't another dead body in our basement or attic or anywhere else."

"Not that I know of, but Detective Bailey would like to meet us at the house for some reason." Ross was wondering as well.

"Great," he muttered. "Why is it I'm not expecting good news?"

"Because the police aren't famous for dispensing that sort of information."

"So the Hotel from Hell has some new secret we don't know about?"

"That's the new name?" He had to stifle a laugh.

"It works for me."

"I'm leaving work now."

"I can do that, but no hint at what this is about?"

"I don't think Bailey hints at anything, so no. Says it outright or doesn't say it at all."

When the call ended, he wrapped up the document he was working on, saved it, and left his office. Whitney had been in meetings all day, so he hadn't talked to her yet and had no idea of her plans for the evening. Hopefully they included him, but it was somewhat of a whirlwind romance, so presuming seemed like a bad idea at this stage.

He sent a text: *Can I buy you a glass of wine this evening?*

She replied at once. *I think I need one, so that's a date. My place?*

I'll bring a bottle, then.

Perfect.

What wasn't perfect was the weather. Dark clouds had gathered and scuttled across the horizon as the wind picked up, and he felt the prick of raindrops as he walked to his car. He slid in and mused it was a perfect atmospheric backdrop for the Demonic Destination, or whatever anyone wanted to call it. Old house that hasn't been lived in in years, a legendary feud, bodies stored behind old organs, bloody floors, dark skies and wind-lashed trees . . .

It truly sounded like a Gothic novel, but at the moment it was reality, and Ross could add to the equation that, for some reason, law enforcement wanted to see him again.

Rain started coming down in earnest. He wished he'd at least looked at the forecast, but it was too late now. If he had to get wet, so be it. He owned an umbrella, but it wasn't with him.

Bailey was there first, which didn't surprise him. The man seemed to be a fairly straightforward cop; if he said he wanted to see you, he expected you to not waste his time. Luckily Cal pulled in behind him.

The new veranda was a bonus as they dashed through the rain. At least the crew had worked on that while the house was considered a crime scene, because none of them showed enthusiasm for going back inside. It was at least solid and safe, and it was progress.

Detective Bailey was, as usual, in his casual attire. "We're going to confiscate some of your property, so I wanted you both to be here."

Whatever Ross expected, it wasn't that. He shook out the moisture from his hair. "We actually have no property here."

"You do, because if it was here when you bought it, it belongs to you along with the house."

Cal looked just as stymied. "Like what?"

"I'll show you."

Of course it was in the basement. He and Cal gave each other a resigned look when Bailey got out a flashlight and led them through the kitchen to the door. It hadn't improved since their last visit — the electrical work hadn't been done yet, so there was still no lighting — except there was no body down there this time. The light shone on two wooden crates in a dank corner.

"Take a look and tell me, please, if you knew they were here." Bailey lifted the lid of one of the containers. "Same thing in the other one."

Guns?

Not exactly what Ross expected. They looked old, too, like they had seen some service, but he was hardly an expert on antique firearms.

"What the hell?" Cal said. "Boxes full of pistols and rifles?"

"Is that confirmation you didn't know they were here?"

Ross was able to say with conviction, "No, we didn't."

Bailey was as hard to read as ever. "They're worth a lot of money, I would guess, and if you didn't store them here, then they're evidence. You can have them back when we figure out where they came from. I suspect it was our victim who put them here, but where did he get them?"

As if he had any idea. Ross shook his head. "Antique weapons aren't my area of expertise."

It wasn't like Cal was an authority either. "I go deer hunting with my dad, and that's about it. No clue here."

"There's every chance, if whoever arranged for the weapons to be stored here has learned Riley is dead, they'll come looking for them. Please understand that we don't know what the arrangement was, but someone brought them here to store them for — I'm speculating — the purpose of selling them. I doubt this person killed Riley, because they would have taken the guns when they did so."

Thunder cracked; even in the basement they could feel it and hear it. The ground shook.

"It isn't a crime to sell old guns, is it?"

"If they're stolen it is, and why else ask someone like Riley to handle them? He was already moving a commodity considered illegal by this state through this property. That is not speculation; that is confirmed."

"I'll warn the construction crew to be careful of anyone coming around. They're already spooked by finding a dead guy." Cal sounded resigned but somber. "Let us help you carry the contraband out."

Of course it was still pouring rain as they emerged with the very heavy boxes. Ross knew he'd have to at least stop at home to change his clothes and grab that promised bottle of wine. All Cal said to him as they hurried to their vehicles was that he would text him so they could talk tomorrow.

Stormy night, more potential trouble on the horizon . . . great. At least he had a date. That was something.

It was too soon, but marriage had crossed his mind. The thought lingered like a ghost in the shadows. It surprised him, but maybe it shouldn't, he mused as he switched on the wipers and his lights. Whitney was both lovely and intelligent and he enjoyed her company. Still a little shy in bed, but he found that surprisingly sexy.

A cache of guns that might have been obtained illegally stored on his property — *that* he didn't find appealing at all.

It sounded like trouble, and that was the last thing he and Cal needed. Even if they were valuable, he wasn't sure he wanted them.

Home. Dry clothes. Wine.

He was going to try and forget about it and focus on the rest of his evening.

* * *

Whitney pulled in and was grateful to see the garage door go up, what with the pounding rain.

Comfortable jeans and her favorite silky blouse made her feel better. She ran a comb through her hair and touched up her lip gloss.

She was looking forward to the evening with Ross.

He arrived about half an hour later, dark hair damp and a little unruly, but that look suited him. Jeans, a button-up shirt, and a bottle of wine in hand as promised, he was every girl's dream, except for the expression on his face.

He looked . . . preoccupied, if she had to define it.

"I'm late. Sorry." The apologetic smile was charming anyway.

"I don't think we set a time. I haven't been home all that long either. Come in and we can listen to the sound of the rain. I'll get two glasses. I had a long day, too."

He lost no time in uncorking the bottle, as if he needed to relax a little. She thought, as they sat down informally in her kitchen, that some of the tension seemed to ease. She hesitated to ask but did anyway. "Is something wrong?"

"Maybe."

"If you want to talk about it, I'm right here."

"I'm not sure I do, to you."

"To me?"

The look in his dark eyes was serious enough it took her aback. He immediately equivocated. "Not because I wouldn't trust you or anything like that, but because it might upset you."

"Pour me some Merlot and just tell me. It's obviously bothering *you*."

Ruby liquid splashed into a glass and he handed it to her. "It is bothering me. Has Will Beeson ever said anything to you about old guns?"

That was an interesting question, but why would it upset her? Whitney paused, thinking it over. "He goes to those Civil War things where they reenact old battles. He likes history, you already know that, so it's no mystery if they interest him. Why?"

"He seems extremely interested in the property Cal and I own, and there are a lot of old guns stored there."

"You're connecting him to both things?" She wasn't sure she understood.

"According to Bailey, those guns could be worth a lot of money. Quite a few murders have been connected to that house, and several are recent."

"And you're implying Will Beeson might be part of it?" She was incredulous.

"I'm wondering."

She took a sip from her glass and set it down. "Are you serious?"

Apparently he was. "He is involved with this somehow. I believe he sent me that book, and I think those guns might belong to him. He knew the house was empty, and when you told him about the project, he immediately became interested."

Her mind rejected the implication. "You're just guessing. I think law enforcement calls it speculating, and they frown on it."

"You're right. I can't prove it. There are just a few small things that have caught my attention."

"Like what?" She was genuinely curious, because she thought Ross was intellectual enough to never come to such a conclusion without some inner conviction.

"He mentioned to me he collected antique guns and had a family connection to the house." Ross took a sip of wine and looked thoughtful. "It was casual, but almost *too* casual,

214

like he was testing what I knew. It was more the tone of the conversation . . . so you're right, speculation."

Considering she'd gone over the plans with him, it was true Will would know he had time to remove the guns if they were his, but . . . it seemed so far-fetched that the nice man she worked with would be caught up in anything criminal. "He's asked me some questions, too." She said it slowly. "He wanted to be part of the process and know how it was going."

He was also stopping by her office more often.

"Maybe the flowers were just an excuse to ask a few questions, and not an indication of romantic interest, considering it from this angle." Ross looked grim. "Not that I would blame him if he had that interest in you, but there could be other motivation."

"He certainly drives an expensive car, but he is a partner in the firm. I don't know how much his salary is. Otherwise, I don't know anything about his lifestyle." She had to acknowledge that reality.

Ross dangled his glass between his fingers, gently swirling the liquid. "Think about it. He might have the connections to find those valuable antique guns and then to sell them. He's really into the historical society thing."

"So are other people."

They just looked at each other.

"I have to at least tell Bailey."

"It doesn't mean the guns are stolen," she argued.

"No, it doesn't. Except they were stored in an abandoned house and two men have been murdered there recently. The sheriff's department took them away, because, even to my uneducated eye, they did look valuable."

Wouldn't that be ironic, people killing each other over firearms? "It does sound off-key." It was a reluctant admission.

"He might not have been worried about it yet, because through you, he could know what was going on."

He had a point. Casting backward, she wondered how much of the interest had been kindness and how much had been self-serving. Will was smart; that wasn't in question.

But so was Ross. Those flowers had been a mistake.

"Why would he draw attention to the house by sending you the book if those guns are his?"

"I think they were stored there because it was safe and convenient, but not too easy to move. Physically, it would be hard for just one man. It took Cal and me, plus Bailey, to load them in his truck."

None of them were small men, and they were all young and athletic. "Really? That's a lot of guns."

"That's a lot of money."

"How can you know?"

"They're not just old, they're antique and therefore collectable. I don't have to be an expert to figure that out."

"How valuable?"

"That I don't know, but I bet Will Beeson could tell us."

She didn't want to believe he was right, but she did.

CHAPTER TWENTY-SEVEN

I believe a quest for vengeance over a wrong that can't be righted is a futile, useless endeavor. I explained it in an unheard voice a thousand times, but like an avalanche begins with the mere dislodging of a trickle of snow, the force builds and becomes out of control, rolling onward.

My landslide cost many lives, some innocent and some not so innocent. Unfortunately, I think I belong to the latter group.

And yet, for all of my regrets, I still long for Rose.

* * *

There was no such thing as an ordinary morning now, was there? Chris had showered and dressed, only to go downstairs and find a two-year-old feeding half of her cereal to the dog, using the same spoon she was using, and no adult in sight.

A mouthful for her, and a mouthful for the moppet.

Not his area of expertise.

He did not know how to scold a child. "Chloe, uh, no. I don't think you should do that."

Thankfully, Loretta came in then and took over. "Don't feed the puppy from your bowl." She looked resigned. "Sorry, I had to go to the bathroom and thought she'd be fine for one minute."

"No problem, the moppet was happy with the arrangement." He let her handle it and left for work, resigned that instead of a decent cup of coffee, he'd have to drink some of the witch's brew Lawrence preferred at the office.

Doreen was, of course, at her desk — proof again that she never left it. "Morning, darlin'," she murmured as he walked through the door. "There's a note on your desk."

Wonderful. "From our favorite friend?"

"He's quite polite. He calls me Miss Doreen."

"I don't suggest accepting a dinner invitation. Just a cautionary note, since he might be a murderer."

"Noted. A woman also called and asked if you'd be in this morning."

"Did she mention why?"

Her phone rang then, and she reached for it. "Nope."

He went to his desk and, indeed, saw the note in her looping handwriting sitting on his computer keyboard.

Have you found him yet?

That directed him right back to his original conversation with whoever this person might be. Who the hell was he looking for? Oh, he'd found some victims recently, but apparently not the right one.

Not six feet deep. That message had certainly been cryptic.

Both Riley and Johnson qualified, but why was it he was still convinced there was a third body out there? If Riley had been killed during a dispute over the weed distribution by Frank Williams — who was, thankfully, still alive as of this morning — what accounted for the second murder?

But it didn't seem like he had any reason to kill Johnson, and that murder was eerily similar to how, long ago, Richard Maddox had been killed, according to the history of the feud connected to the house.

The woman who walked through the door just then must have been in tune with his thoughts, because he glanced up and recognized her. Cal Nolte's sister, smooth blonde hair and a slender but shapely figure — she was memorable even in a dark house with blood-splattered floors.

Naturally, Doreen pointed her in his direction. He stood politely to gesture at the chair by his desk. "Ms. Nolte, what can I do for you?"

"I don't know." She sat and her expression was definitely troubled. "I also don't know if I'm doing the right thing or not, but I thought maybe I should tell you, since Ross talked to me about the guns."

Waylan and not her brother? Interesting, but they were working together, and for all he knew, a couple. "Information is always appreciated."

"I have an associate that collects old guns and has some sort of family connection to the house. The next property over belongs to his nephew, who inherited it from his grandfather, who owned the whole parcel. Ross thinks the guns might be there because of him. I don't want to be the one to suggest you investigate him, but he has done some odd things lately."

His nephew? This might be the break he was looking for, the one that could make this case finally hang together. Chris chose to not mention he might have had a possible fatal confrontation with the nephew yesterday afternoon. "Do you know his nephew's name?"

"Last name, no." She lifted her shoulders in apology. "Will just mentioned him now and then. Frank, I think, for the first name."

That was significant. So Williams was possibly tied to the guns, and most certainly to the illegal transportation of the marijuana — not to mention being responsible for the death of Riley, if that could be proven. He'd all but admitted it by trying to draw his weapon on a law enforcement officer.

"I think we've met."

His dry tone registered, and her eyes widened. "You and Frank?"

"Can I have the full name of this associate, so I can look into this?"

"I brought one of his business cards. I don't have his home address. We work together but don't socialize, other than at office events." She set it on his desk — reluctantly, he could tell. "I've always thought he was a nice man and I'm not convinced he isn't, but there's enough doubt that I'm here, I guess."

"Disclosure is not the usual way of doing my job, unless it's mandated by the court. Your visit here won't be mentioned."

"Thank you." She looked relieved.

He didn't blame her. Being the one to point a finger was never a pleasant experience, especially if you liked the person in question, even if perhaps they weren't quite the person you thought they were. "We appreciate you coming in."

After she left, he went to see Lawrence. "May I have a word?"

"Oh no, here comes trouble." The sheriff ran his fingers through his graying hair, leaning back in his chair. "Son, as far as I know, that foolhardy boy is still breathing. I hope he continues to. I have a few questions for him once he can answer them."

It was good to hear. Chris said, "That's something, anyway, but not why I'm here. I'm going to check out one of those old sidearms and a rifle we seized and take them to be appraised. I have an unexpected lead. We'll see if it works out to be something."

"Try not to shoot anyone this afternoon, as a favor to me, Bailey. The thought of you with two weapons makes me want a glass of bourbon."

"I believe I'm supposed to carry a weapon and was trained to use it if necessary." He wasn't being defensive, just pointing it out.

"All true." Lawrence was a pragmatic man. He folded his hands together. "So follow your lead, Detective."

"Will do."

Carter was out on a case, but Chris wanted to do this alone anyway, so he went down, signed off on the guns and put them in his truck. Then he went in to sit back at his desk and try to figure out how to lie without actually telling a lie.

He finally settled on not mentioning his occupation and just saying someone he knew mentioned Mr. Beeson was an expert on antique guns, and that he wondered if he could maybe date the ones he had.

So he made the call to the number on the card.

And Chris very much recognized the voice that answered.

* * *

Cal came into his office bringing lunch, and at least some good news. He set down the box with the sandwiches and drinks on Ross's desk. "The crew is back inside tearing apart the kitchen. Apparently drugs and guns are far less scary than a possible murderous ghost. A quick explanation seemed to take care of it. I ordered the new cabinets this morning."

Ross was at least happy to hear that. But his conversation with Whitney was weighing on his mind, no doubt about that. "Have you met Will Beeson?"

"Partner in her firm? I think once when I went to her office. Older guy, right?" Cal was nothing but quick. "Why?"

"I've talked to him about the house because of the historical designation, and he has a family connection to it somehow."

"That's helpful."

"He's also into collectable antique guns and is carefully monitoring our progress on the restoration."

Cal put down his sandwich and looked at him in consternation. "So you think those might be *his* guns?"

"Maybe. He's been dropping by Whitney's office and checking on where the project is at, on one excuse or another. I think maybe he was trying to figure out how to get them out of there to another location before anyone found them and realized their value."

There was no doubt Cal was unconvinced. "Now, that would be a coincidence I'd find hard to believe. We buy a house and hire my sister as the architect, and one of the associates in her office is hiding stolen property in the basement?"

"Not that much of a coincidence. It's a historic house, he knew it was empty, and it used to be in his family. When we bought it, Whitney asked him about it because we wanted to keep the historical designation, and he's active in the society. Suddenly his convenient storage place for the weapons belonged to someone else, and he had an inside line on a time frame to get them out of there." Ross had really been thinking it over, once he'd said it out loud to Whitney.

"So you think he's a cog in a wheel marketing stolen guns?"

"Maybe. If they were obtained legally, why store them in the basement of an old uninhabited house? There were a lot of weapons in those heavy boxes."

"True. I'm glad I work out, because those stairs weren't much of a picnic."

"The sheriff's office seemed to take an interest."

"Yes, they did," Cal agreed, not looking happy about it. "At least Detective Bailey seemed to take our word for it we never put them there."

"Well, we didn't put the dead man in the basement either, and he seemed to not consider us suspects. Yeah, I'm pretty happy about that, too." Ross paused, weighing his next words, undecided whether or not he should even say them. "I'm thinking of asking Whitney to marry me."

The abrupt change in subject obviously threw Cal off. He choked on his last bite, then finally swallowed. It was a little theatrical; Ross gave him a telling look. "Don't look so damned surprised."

"How am I supposed to look? You're thinking about it? That isn't a real commitment yet, is it?"

It was hard to admit, but he had a point. Ross sat back and lifted his hands. "Okay, not well put. We haven't been involved that long, but my impression is she's as cautious about relationships as I am. What if she says no?"

"Are you really asking me this?"

* * *

It wasn't that Cal wasn't happy Ross was finally serious. But Ross's insecurity was just plain amusing on a certain level, because he was a very self-confident man. Cal had to laugh.

Ross looked annoyed. "Like hell I'd joke about this."

"I don't know, since you've never been serious before."

"Aren't you supposed to be serious once only, and hope it works out?"

That was a valid point. "Yes. You're dating my sister, and I'm dating her good friend, and it's proof we're both idiots or else extremely intelligent. As for your question, I don't know. That's up to her, and how to deal with a refusal is out of the realm of my experience when it comes to marriage. Whitney is pretty independent and always has been."

But, if they were sleeping together, she was serious as well. He knew she was not at all promiscuous, quite the opposite. That Ross could manage to seduce her didn't really surprise him, but that *he'd* fallen hard enough to consider marriage did.

"She'll say yes." Cal set aside his napkin and rose. "I know her, and I've seen you together. I was afraid she'd want more than you were willing to give, and I'm happy I was wrong. Been shopping for a ring yet?"

"I've stopped briefly at that jeweler downtown, just to look."

Cal's brows went up. That meant he really was ready to do the on-bended-knee thing. "If you want a second opinion, let me know and I'll go with you. Good practice for maybe a future effort on my part."

Ross smiled briefly. "Thanks, and thanks for lunch, too . . . What the hell are we going to do with those guns, if they're returned to us?"

That was a good question. He didn't have an answer. "Don't know. At this point, to quote my grandmother's favorite saying, let's cross that bridge when we come to it. I'm just happy to have them out of the house and the construction crew back in it."

"Who knows what else might be in the haunted basement?" Ross blew out a short breath. "We have to get rid of that cursed organ, we have dozens of boxes down there containing who knows what, and I'm guessing you and I have to be the ones to look through it all."

"I'm guessing you're right. We'll probably find body parts, shrunken heads, that sort of thing."

"Yeah, that's also my prediction based on the way things have gone so far."

Cal left, inwardly laughing but not arguing. Nothing had gone exactly according to plan, yet he was still all about the idea, and at the moment, happy for Whitney and Ross. He'd never considered himself a romantic, but maybe he was wrong.

As far as the house went, it was certainly keeping its history intact.

CHAPTER TWENTY-EIGHT

As events unfold, it is easy to look back and second-guess your decisions.
Like aforethought, afterthought is also an entity.

* * *

Nice office. Pleasant secretary who duly pointed him to the right door, though she did look at his duffle bag with curiosity.

Chris didn't want to explain, but he thought of it as fishing tackle — bait for possible information on antique weapons and who might market them.

Beeson's office door was open. Chris rapped on the doorframe first and was greeted with an affable smile from a man maybe in his early fifties or so, sitting behind a very nice oak desk.

Chris merely said, "Mr. Beeson, good morning. I'm Chris. I called you. Thank you for agreeing to look at the guns." He deliberately didn't introduce himself with his last name. He had his badge, of course, but discreetly tucked into his pocket.

"No problem. Old weapons are a particular hobby of mine."

Chris took a seat in a leather chair. "So I heard, but I appreciate your time. If you can value these for me and give me some possible history on them, that would be great. I tried online and have a vague historical perspective, but just need someone who knows more about it, because I'm clueless as to value."

"Let's see what you have."

He opened the bag and took out the revolver first, setting it on the desk.

Beeson picked it up and examined it. "Colt Dragoon. Made before the Civil War, starting in the 1850s. Worth quite a lot, as it is a nice one in good condition. A great piece."

"What does 'quite a lot' mean?"

"You'd be pleasantly surprised, given the right buyer. You heard about me how?"

"We have a mutual acquaintance."

That was evasive, but Chris already wondered if Beeson recognized his voice. He certainly had his, especially now that they were face to face. He took out the rifle. "What about this one?"

"A Remington. The company was established in 1816, and this is an older model a collector would want. Where did you get these?" He gave an inquiring look.

"Out of an old basement."

There was a sudden flicker of wary acknowledgement in Beeson's eyes. "I see."

"So they're valuable?" His tone was deliberate.

"Indeed they are."

"What body will I never find?"

It took a moment, but Beeson responded with impressive composure. "Detective Bailey, it is a pleasure to meet you in person."

"So you know who I am and why I'm here." Chris did his best to sound neutral. "You initiated the contact. Care to tell me why?"

He sat back, a faint ironic smile on his mouth. "You've already gained quite a reputation for your deductive powers, for such a young man."

And that meant what? Chris wasn't into playing games this way. "Was Johnson killed because he knew about the guns and wanted to cash in on them? We did find his body, and it certainly wasn't six feet deep. I'm having a hard time comprehending why you would bring it to my attention."

"I'm not admitting to anything, Detective. You came here to see me, and I evaluated some firearms."

"You do realize Doreen could identify your voice? I did."

"So? It doesn't prove I've committed any crime, does it?"

"No, but your nephew certainly isn't innocent."

"He isn't my responsibility. He's a grown man."

"No, but you were both using the house illegally."

"Prove it."

So, Anna was right; this was a challenge. He just had to wonder what triggered it and why he had become involved. The fatal shooting last year in a triple homicide case — where two police officers, himself included, had been shot — had drawn a lot of press, and not just local. Maybe that had inspired it, who knew?

Chris sat back. "I can prove, through the DEA and an inspection of the property he owns, Frank was growing a plant that at this time is still illegal in this state. I can prove he was selling it to distributors. And I can prove, probably beyond a reasonable doubt, that he killed the man named Riley, who we found in the cellar of that house, because they got into an argument over this business. As for you, where did you get the guns?"

"I'm not sure what you're talking about, Detective Bailey." Beeson looked composed.

"Did Johnson want a cut?"

"From what, the proceeds of said guns you think I know about?"

"Just asking a straightforward question."

"You do seem like a straightforward kind of man."

"I certainly hope so. That is part of my job."

"I can be direct, too. You think I killed him."

This was one of the most interesting interviews he'd done, most certainly. "I'm wondering if you didn't have the incentive and opportunity to do so."

"You have no proof."

"Except maybe the phone calls to me."

"That is as circumstantial as it gets."

The man was right, of course. However, Chris could connect him to the house, and his expertise in antique guns might build something of a case; circumstantial evidence could weigh with a jury. But Beeson was correct in that he couldn't prove in the least that Johnson knew the guns were there or had made an attempt to take any of them. At this point, no district attorney would agree to charge him with any of it.

Except Chris had the knife.

It was definitely old. The case was building in his mind

. . .

That was Beeson's real mistake, if Chris could trace it. Antique guns and a unique ornate knife? It wasn't hard evidence.

A prosecutor *might* look at that. Maybe. It might be more than Chris saying — even with Doreen as backup — that the voice was familiar.

He rose. "I appreciate your time."

"That's it, Detective?"

"For now."

He left, thinking it over. Johnson was in bed with both Williams and Beeson, helping them out by not listing the house until he was forced to by Ross Waylan's inquiry. The only reason an agent would come back to the house after it was sold and the closing was done was to maybe take something valuable he knew was there. That would explain it, but it was speculation. One of them killed him, and based on the conversation he'd had, probably Beeson. He hadn't admitted or denied anything.

Chris wasn't positive who was the cat or who was the mouse in that exchange.

Neither had either one of them mentioned the hope-fully-not-fatal shooting of Frank Williams. Maybe Beeson didn't know.

Or maybe he did. Their conversation had been on the combative side. He wasn't sure he'd ever had someone ask him outright if he suspected them of murder.

The truth of the matter was, he did.

* * *

It was late afternoon when Ross walked through the door of her office with a bouquet of flowers and an ironic smile. Whitney raised her eyebrows, and it registered with him. He said, "I probably should have made a romantic gesture before this."

"You've been very romantic." The flowers were lovely, an exotic mixture of blooms; some she could identify and some she didn't know offhand.

"Physically, but not sentimentally."

"I beg to differ. You've told me you're in love with me. That's extremely sentimental."

He set down the bouquet on her desk. "I'm going to ask you to marry me. What are we going to do for dinner?"

That declaration coming out so casually gave her pause. Ross didn't do anything without thought, so the cavalier approach didn't fool her. "You are?"

"Wondering about dinner? Of course. Everyone has to eat."

"Ross." There was reproof in her tone. He deserved it, in her opinion.

Mildly, he said, "I was just warning you so you could think it over."

"Isn't that the same as asking?"

He looked so striking with his loosened tie and wavy hair, which was never perfect but suited him, like he should grace the cover of some romance novel. "Maybe," he equiv-ocated. "If so, what do you think you would say?"

Her answer was negated by the interruption of a cool voice. "Nice flowers, Mr Waylan. A gallant gesture. Why am I not surprised to find you here? It is fortuitous to find you together, because I wanted to ask which one of you told Detective Bailey I was an expert on old guns."

No threat. The same normal demeanor, but Whitney felt an unexpected chill. It could be, she told herself, she wasn't looking at the mild-mannered Will Beeson she thought she knew.

"I did." She volunteered the information. "He's investigating the murder of someone found in the basement of the house my brother bought. He found a lot of guns that might have historical value, and he had questions. I referred him to you."

There was palpable tension in the room. She could see it in both men. Will finally said, "I see. That explains it, then."

He left abruptly, and she looked at Ross. "Ah, that was awkward."

"It was. You're coming home with me."

Maybe she shouldn't have gone to Bailey. "I have to admit perhaps I did the wrong thing."

"Or not." He spoke emphatically. "But in any case, we're going home together."

The autocratic tone would have irritated her, but he was right. Something was off. She picked up the flowers. "I'll sign off on my computer and let's go. I'm done for the day, anyway."

Ross didn't look happy at all as he walked her to her car. "I'll follow you. I'm hardly trained in psychology, but I can tell when another male is pissed off. Beeson didn't conceal it well."

She stopped by the driver's side of her car. "If he's innocent of any wrongdoing, he has nothing to worry about."

"Our problem is, I don't think that's the case."

She'd come to the same conclusion. "He's not acting at all normal."

"I don't know him well enough to determine that, but he seems unhappy to me. Get in and I'll follow and—"

The car came out of nowhere. It hit Ross first, and then he slammed into her, both of them pinned to her car. Then the vehicle backed up and drove away.

Over in a moment.

They both collapsed to the pavement. She wasn't even quite sure at first what had happened, Whitney was so dazed. She scrambled up and touched Ross's face.

He didn't move at first, and she panicked until he groaned and opened his eyes. "Oh shit. That hurt."

At least he wasn't unconscious.

"I'm calling 911." She'd dropped her purse, and with shaking hands found it.

"I don't think I'm going to die or anything. You cushioned the impact." He moved, holding his right arm, struggling to sit up and failing. "Are you hurt?"

"The car didn't actually hit *me*."

"*I* certainly hit you. Maybe you should call Bailey instead and tell him Beeson has lost his mind."

It had been his car. She'd caught a glimpse of it before it hit Ross, but luckily, there hadn't been enough space for it to gain any real speed; still, the impact had been significant enough.

"I don't know if I need an ambulance, but I might have a broken arm. Note to self: putting out your hand does not stop a vehicle from hitting you."

She called the emergency services. A police report wouldn't hurt, and if Ross's arm was broken, he'd need medical attention. Plus, he could have other injuries.

"There's a hit-and-run and we need medical attention." After she gave the address, she registered there was blood pooling on the ground and knelt next to him. "Ross, how bad is it?"

"I'm guessing compound fracture. I can feel the bone sticking out. And my hip . . . I can't stand up."

Worse than she thought. "If I knew what to do, I'd do it. I'm not a nurse or doctor. I don't want to hurt you more."

"You called and they'll get here. It could be worse."

She still couldn't believe it had happened. "Why would Will do that?"

"He's running scared, or something else is going on. I think he just tried to kill two people. I'm serious, take my phone and call Bailey. I don't think I can reach it. Left pocket of my shirt."

* * *

Chris was making a left turn onto the street that led to his house when he answered his phone.

"Bailey."

Female voice, uneven but not quite hysterical. "This is Whitney Nolte. I'm not sure what triggered this, but William Beeson just hit Ross deliberately with his car. We're waiting on the ambulance."

That wasn't exactly wonderful news. He was trying to solve a murder, not be a catalyst for another one. "Where are you?"

"In the parking lot of our office."

"I'm on my way back. If the ambulance gets there before me, you'll see me at the hospital, so you can tell me exactly what happened."

This could be his fault for pointing out to Beeson he was a suspect in the Johnson murder, which was the truth, but he hadn't intended to send him over some edge. If his suspicion was right, Beeson had stepped off the precipice before. Hitting someone with a car was an act of rage, but so was plunging a dagger into their chest and tossing their body into a small lake.

He'd been on the right trail, but with no proof except the antique dagger connection. Now he had an eyewitness to an actual crime. This case had just broken.

He pulled into a driveway and turned around so swiftly his tires screeched. He backed out and headed toward where he'd just left.

The ambulance had just arrived when he got there ten minutes later. Ross Waylan didn't look all that great as they lifted him onto the stretcher. There was blood on his shirt, his arm was taped to his chest, and he was ghostly pale.

Chris would just as soon skip being hit by a car, even if it was a really expensive one. He had to give Whitney Nolte credit; she was holding it together, and she wasn't unscathed, either. There was a cut on her forehead, and when he walked over, she was visibly shaken. "You can ride with them and I'll follow if you want."

"I'm more in shock than injured."

"You take a double hit when someone you trust deliberately hurts someone you care about." He wasn't trying to be philosophical, but it was true. Worst kind of betrayal. "So you know it was Beeson's car?"

She didn't hesitate. "Yes. Absolutely. I saw the license plate — ARC 1969. I see it every day. Plus, it isn't like I don't know his car."

That was solid information.

He was going to arrest Mr. Beeson on at least a hit-and-run, and hopefully Lawrence would back attempted murder. When it came to Johnson, if he could trace the knife, it would be a murder case.

Of course, at that moment, his phone rang.

It was Doreen. "Bailey, I need you."

She almost never called him by his last name. Something was wrong, he could hear it in her voice. "Fine. I'm having an interesting evening already . . . can I ask why?"

"Come *now*."

She hung up, and he knew he needed to go. Doreen didn't do anything lightly. "That was an emergency call." For what, he wasn't sure. He turned his attention back to Whitney Nolte. "If you aren't sure you can drive, then don't."

"I'm sure." Her self-possession was coming back.

He believed her, which was good, because he was off to his truck at a dead run.

Luckily, it wasn't far to the sheriff's office, and he arrived swiftly — maybe breaking the speed limits, but he was an officer and allowed some latitude.

What he walked into was certainly not expected. Body on the floor in front of the main desk where Doreen sat, blood in a pool around it. She looked ashen but resolute.

"What the hell happened?"

She took in an audible breath. "I knew him. I recognized his voice."

In his entire tenure with the sheriff's office, he'd never seen her shaken. By way of explanation, she said succinctly, "He wanted those damn guns you brought here. I told him they were in lockup, and he took out a gun and pointed it at me and told me to get them. I said I would get the keys, got my gun instead out of my desk drawer, and I shot him. Then I wasn't sure what to do next, so I called you."

"I'll get this." He hoped he sounded reassuring. "This could be my fault."

Well, *shit*. It really could be.

Beeson. He knelt and searched for a pulse, wondering how this particular day had dissolved into utter chaos.

"Is he dead?" Her voice quavered a little.

"Not yet." There was a pulse, but it was faint. "You need to call, but this makes it a lot easier for me to arrest him."

"I'm not going to apologize to anyone for shooting him." She reached for the phone.

"I doubt anyone would ask you to. He tried to kill someone earlier, and you have every right to protect yourself."

"He did?"

"Just call."

CHAPTER TWENTY-NINE

In my final moments, I believe I faced desperation. I'd never seen it before, so it was new to me. No one was so determined to escape the truth of the circumstances. We'd fought a battle and he'd lost.

But, I suppose, in the end, he won.

No, not true. I think we both lost.

* * *

It really was not the best evening of his life. Who would think bringing flowers to a pretty woman would be such a dangerous endeavor?

An MRI showed that besides his arm woes, Ross had a fractured pelvic bone from the impact, but according to the orthopedic doctor, it was hairline and didn't require surgery. The arm they put back in place, so he had an elaborate rigid sling and stitches. The only other result was going to be some healthy bruises. All in all, Ross was informed, he was a lucky man.

He *felt* lucky when Whitney came in and the first thing she did was kiss him. That was fine with him; he was battered but okay otherwise. Certainly well enough to appreciate the brush of her hair and the softness of her lips.

"Bailey was here and I described what happened. I have no idea what he's going to do next, but I feel like he has some insight into this we don't."

"I hope so." That was a heartfelt sentiment. "Obviously Beeson has lost it for some reason. I don't know if it was because I brought you flowers, or because you told Bailey about him." Or a combination of both, he thought grimly. Something set him off.

"I doubt he's actually jealous."

The only good news was that with probably both a shortage of beds and the fact that he was really a repair job, the doctor said yes to him being released. He listened to the instructions and signed with his good hand and went outside gratefully. In a wheelchair, but still.

Whitney held his uninjured arm and opened the passenger door for him. Getting in was awkward, but he managed it. When she slid into the driver's seat, she said abruptly, "I think Will has a mental problem."

"You mean the man who tried to kill me with his car?" He didn't want to be sarcastic, but truthfully his arm really hurt, even with the meds.

"No, listen to me. He's been slipping for a while. Asking about projects that were finished, and getting short if you corrected him and pointed out they'd been done for some time. It wasn't bad, but I noticed it. There's psychosis that involves a confusion of present-day and past events, whether in your own life or history."

He stared at her. "You've looked into this?"

"I wondered, so I read about it."

She was serious. He wasn't too surprised, because Whitney was smart, not just lovely from head to toe. "He seemed lucid to me when I talked to him."

"He's very . . . focused. Intelligent, yes, but out of touch at times. He's obsessed with the past, which is why I thought he could help you with the house."

Beeson had actually been a font of information, but he'd also sent him that book, Ross was sure of it now. "I don't know, but he obviously took exception to Bailey's visit."

"I don't know either." She hadn't escaped unscathed, but a nurse had treated the injury on her forehead and they had checked to make sure she didn't have broken ribs. Thankfully not, because Ross would have blamed himself, and even he hadn't slammed into her intentionally, he would feel terrible.

She drove slowly, probably in deference to his injuries, her expression troubled. "This all feels very surreal to me."

"I agree. I'm still worried about dinner."

At least she laughed. "Ross."

"I have a broken arm and various other bruised parts," he said mildly. "I shouldn't have to be hungry too."

"I'll make sure we eat, and by the way, yes."

He sent her an inquiring look.

"I will most definitely say yes if you ask me to marry you."

Well, maybe it wasn't such a bad evening after all.

* * *

"Why is everyone in this office shooting people?"

Lawrence was rattled, Chris realized. "Sir, I would have done the same thing."

"Oh, I know you would. You did it yesterday. We aren't in an old-time saloon, son, but there's blood on my floor and an ambulance pulling away."

Well, if nothing else, he was going to stand in Doreen's corner. "What was she supposed to do? He was threatening her. That same man tried to kill someone else in a hit-and-run tonight."

At least the sheriff was a reasonable man, once he settled down. He blew out a short breath. "I agree. No one should be able to come into this office and wave a gun around or deliberately try to run someone over. Just tell me what the hell you think went wrong."

"I'm not sure."

"Oh, that's my favorite answer."

Doreen picked up the baton. She had rallied since the event. "Detective Bailey isn't at fault. Those guns were evidence at a potential crime scene, and I wasn't giving them to some stranger. That would be not doing my job. He pointed a gun at me and I pointed one back."

Lawrence, of course, listened to her. It took him a moment but he conceded. "I understand. I'll just have to justify it all to the public. I'm glad neither one of you were injured and kept cool heads in both incidents. Now, as long as Carter or one of the deputies doesn't feel the urge to drop someone in their tracks this evening, I'm going back home."

Chris waited until he'd left then looked at Doreen. "That actually went better than I thought it would."

"I don't know about you, but I'm going home too, but for a tall cocktail and maybe some reruns of old comedies. I hate to tell you this, but the young man you shot really wants to talk to you."

He'd planned on going home to Anna and his inadvertently adopted family, who might all be actually safe now. "What?"

"Before all this happened, the hospital called twice. He wants you to come visit him. Frank Williams? He has something to tell you."

"And here I thought I could catch a break. What could he possibly have to tell me?"

"You'd have to go and see."

"You have to be kidding me."

"I'm not in a humorous mood this evening, Detective."

He accepted that. Doreen didn't tend to pull punches.

EPILOGUE

The location of the old well was exactly where he'd been told it would be. It was in a desolate corner behind the house with overgrown trees guarding it.

Chris found it easily enough.

Hand-dug years ago, it had been abandoned for a century at least.

"So now what do we do? Get Search and Rescue?"

Carter wore a white shirt, but this time, a lavender tie. Very whimsical attire for a man with such a sharp and pragmatic outlook on not just law enforcement but life in general. "SAR's a logical choice. You and I aren't going down that hole. Tell me again what Williams said."

"He told me that his uncle Will said when his grandfather disappeared about fifteen years ago, and I'm quoting, 'He might have fallen down a long hole with water at the bottom.' My impression is, he's thought all along Will Beeson killed his own father."

"What a warm and loving family."

"I did check. His wife reported him missing."

Hands in his pockets, Carter looked contemplative. "If we find bones down there, Beeson will have lost yet again."

"He's an unstable man. Whitney Nolte told me she thinks he has problems separating the present from his fascination with the past. Maybe she has a handle on it. I doubt we'll be able to prove it based on the word of another murderer, but if there are bones down there and DNA comes through that it's a match, then the case gets stronger against either one of them."

"So Williams wants a plea bargain. He gave us a cold case we can strike off the books in exchange for a manslaughter charge instead of murder."

Chris nodded as they walked back to the car. "He said he knew Riley was taking a bigger cut from the drug deals than what they'd agreed on and finally confronted him about it. It turned physical, but Williams swears it was self-defense. He took the body over to the old house and hid it because he didn't know what else to do with it."

"He told all this to the police officer that shot him?" Carter looked skeptical.

"I helped Kyle out, and I told Williams not to reach for his weapon. I think I seem like a fair man, and he's trying to go for that angle."

"It's up to the prosecutor how to charge him."

That was true enough, and Chris had listened to what Williams had to say. But the fact remained he'd arrived at Chris's residence armed and with something in mind.

Carter opened his door, but didn't get in, just looked at him for a moment over the top of the car. "So you're leaving for the Feds."

They had to have this conversation sooner or later. Chris nodded. "I have a date and a time."

"Damn, a new partner. I was just getting used to you."

"Lawrence is aware, so he might be looking around. Maybe he'll give you Doreen."

"Well, she seems to already be following in your footsteps."

Beeson had lived, but it was a narrow escape. His obsession with old weapons had caught up with him, because in an effort to find out why those guns were so important, they had found that he'd been interested in antique knives as well. A search of his house, courtesy of a warrant, revealed several like the murder weapon used on Johnson and left at the cabin. It wasn't definitive evidence, but it would probably be enough, given the location of where the weapons were found, and the fact that he was looking for the guns desperately enough he was willing to point a gun at a woman *in* the sheriff's office.

The old house connection, his questionable mental state, and his erratic actions — the district attorney agreed there was enough to charge him with Johnson's murder. Not a slam dunk by any means, but even without direct physical evidence, solid enough. Means, motive, and opportunity.

Two cases closed, maybe three, if Williams was to be believed.

But there was one more thing on his plate.

Chris still had to tell Anna he was leaving. He didn't know if he'd be assigned to an office in Tennessee or not once he was done with training.

Except it turned out he didn't have to, because she obviously already knew somehow. Carter dropped him off and he walked into a quiet house off, except for the moppet. Everyone was gone, and there was a note on the counter.

Congratulations. Maybe someday I'll wake up next to you again.

Well, that was fair enough. Goodbye for now, but not forever.

He'd take that.

THE END

THE JOFFE BOOKS STORY

We began in 2014 when Jasper agreed to publish his mum's much-rejected romance novel and it became a bestseller.

Since then we've grown into the largest independent publisher in the UK. We're extremely proud to publish some of the very best writers in the world, including Joy Ellis, Faith Martin, Caro Ramsay, Helen Forrester, Simon Brett and Robert Goddard. Everyone at Joffe Books loves reading and we never forget that it all begins with the magic of an author telling a story.

We are proud to publish talented first-time authors, as well as established writers whose books we love introducing to a new generation of readers.

We have been shortlisted for Independent Publisher of the Year at the British Book Awards three times, in 2020, 2021 and 2022, and for the Diversity and Inclusivity Award at the Independent Publishing Awards in 2022.

We built this company with your help, and we love to hear from you, so please email us about absolutely anything bookish at: feedback@joffebooks.com.

If you want to receive free books every Friday and hear about all our new releases, join our mailing list: www.joffebooks.com/contact

And when you tell your friends about us, just remember: it's pronounced Joffe as in coffee or toffee!